Jessie

the story of a genteel
lady in frontier Alaska

as told by

Betty Wyatt

Jessie: the story of a genteel lady in frontier Alaska

This book is a work based on historical fact.　　Some　persons　named really lived, and most events really happened. Unverifiable details have been embellished by the author's imagination.

Book cover design by Patricia Slack
Maps by John Wyatt

ISBN—978-1-4303-0905-5

DEDICATED TO

The "Love of My Life" – John, who continues to amaze me with his God-given talents. I could not begin to list all he has done toward this book: from encouraging my writing to outfitting the car and camper for the road journey of a lifetime to Eagle, Alaska; or from reading the entire manuscript out loud to preparing meals while I visited with folks about "my" project.

And

The genteel Jessie...If only we could have met.

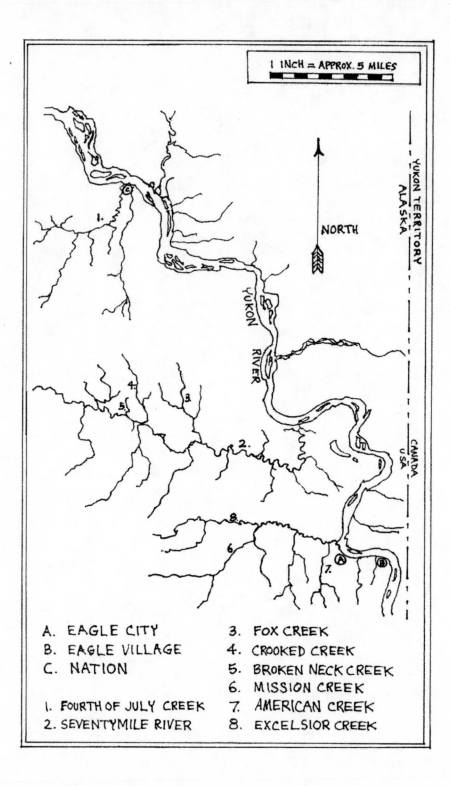

1 INCH = APPROX. 5 MILES

NORTH

YUKON TERRITORY
ALASKA

CANADA
USA

YUKON RIVER

A. EAGLE CITY
B. EAGLE VILLAGE
C. NATION

1. FOURTH OF JULY CREEK
2. SEVENTYMILE RIVER

3. FOX CREEK
4. CROOKED CREEK
5. BROKEN NECK CREEK
6. MISSION CREEK
7. AMERICAN CREEK
8. EXCELSIOR CREEK

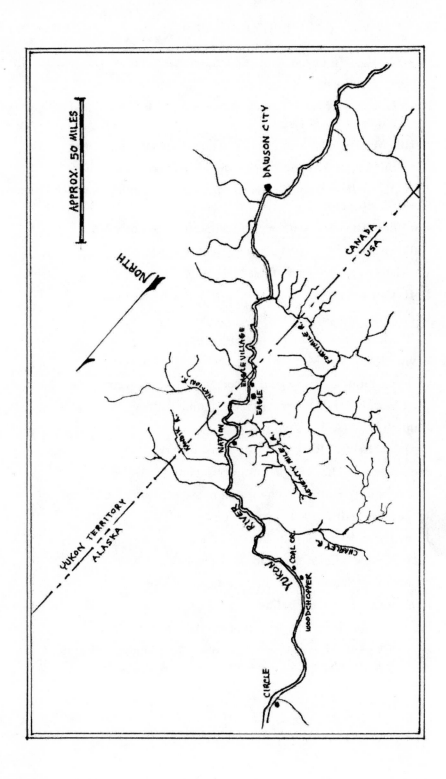

LIST OF CHARACTERS

A. G. & Mrs. Fullerton –Episcopal missionaries (1930-47)

Albert Fox – Jessie's brother; two years her junior

Ann Hobbs Purdy – Friend mentioned in Jessie's diary; subject of popular Alaska novel *Tisha*

Archie Mather – Love of Jessie's life; handyman and miner

Armand Hagen – Archie's placer mining partner

Billy Mitchell – Army Lieutenant in charge of linking Alaska to outside world via telegraph line

Borghild "Ole" Hansen – Best friend; teacher at Eagle Village

Cathryne Knight – Good neighbor; married to Jess Knight

Charley Ott – Co-owner of local mercantile

D. B. Vanderveer–Liaison to Sedro-Woolley investors

Dr. Walter Caughey Fox – Jessie's Father

Ed Biederman – Winter postman for Eagle

Ervin "Twiddles" Mather – A trapper; Archie's uncle

George Matlock – Early gold miner; "colorful" character

Gust Nelson – Gold miner; Archie's mining partner

Hannah Fox – Albert's wife

Herbert "Bertie" Barber– Jessie's first husband

Jack Hillard – U.S. Customs Officer in Eagle

Jess Knight– Northern Commercial Manager; Jessie's neighbor

Jessie Elizabeth Fox – Title character

Jessie Helen Rebecca Ellis Fox – Jessie's Mother

John Scheele – Co-owner of local mercantile

"Nimrod" – "He could make anything but a living."

R. E. Steel – Lawman , politician, roadhouse owner

Rosalind – Jessie's governess and personal maid

Ulysses Grant Myers –Wearer of many hats: mayor, customs Officer, Weather Bureau, excellent dog team owner

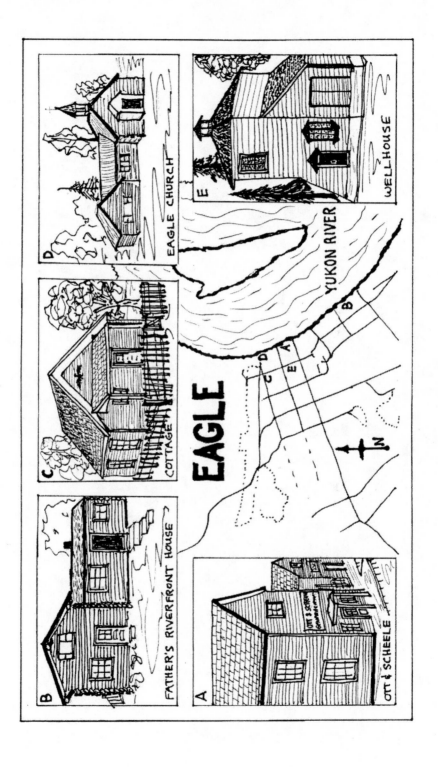

EAGLE

YUKON RIVER

N

A OTT & SCHEELE

B FATHER'S RIVERFRONT HOUSE

C COTTAGE

D EAGLE CHURCH

E WELLHOUSE

PROLOGUE

Climbing to my attic, I know, full well, what I will find – a trunk full of memories...not my own...not even mementoes of anyone I have ever met. And yet, I have stored these treasures of a lady who has been a part of me for more than half my life. I have allowed too many years to pass, and the details about Jessie's life are faded and blended with other memories. I locate a time-browned file folder and peruse its contents. Contained in this folder are the remnants of papers that were in the trunk originally. Included with these papers is my note to the Administrator of the Sitka Pioneer Home.

My connection with the trunk actually began one wintry day in 1969 at the Bureau of Mines in Juneau, Alaska. Who knows why my husband John and I were there? I do know the old glass-fronted library shelves (barrister bookcases) caught his eye; and, learning the office was about to be renovated, he asked how we might be able to acquire them.

"Just put your name on the mailing list for State surplus," the clerk answered. So, that was exactly what we did. Soon, we started receiving the "Closed Bid Auction" notices. Usually in those notices were lists of heavy equipment such as "bulldozer in Nome" with a brief description. Anyone who won the bid was responsible for transporting their newly purchased item from where it sat. In late March 1970, our mailman delivered just such a notice. This time, included on the list was a trunk (contents unknown) in Sitka.

I shared the notice with Joanne on the eve of her departure for a weekend in Sitka and asked, "If you have time to visit the Sitka Pioneer Home, would you check on this trunk?"

Upon her return to Juneau, Joanne called me to say she had gone by the stately Pioneer Home. She said the trunk was stored in a hall closet. It was hard to see its contents because the hall was very dark, but the Administrator had opened the trunk for her. She wasn't certain of what was inside except odds and ends and some Indian things. She had discovered listed in the auction notice another item which caught her attention – an oak desk called a secretary.

Upon notification of being the successful bidders, Joanne and Ron Roberts volunteered to travel to Sitka to collect the purchases. They hand carried the trunk and the secretary onto the Alaska State ferry, and we set a time to divide its trove and treasures. Having peeked at the trunk's contents, Ron warned, "This may be the end of a perfect friendship." Our husbands positioned themselves together with Cheshire-cat grins in order to observe the unraveling of a well-knit comradery.

Meanwhile, we ladies carefully removed each and every item from the trunk and placed it in one of several categories – fine china, baskets, beadwork, what is this thing?, armadillo shell, some journal-appearing books, a British flag. Our living room floor was almost too small a space for this project.

"You choose first." "No, you choose first!" was to be our only argument of the evening. She chose a basket; I chose a basket. I took a plate marked Arctic Brotherhood Camp Eagle No. 13; she took its twin. We decided to not split up the china. I kept most of the china since I would be the keeper of the trunk. We also decided to not divide the personal books; they would be kept together. As it turned out, those four books were a diary, a journal (of sorts), a postcard album, and a photo album.

As we were beginning to set things back in the trunk, one of us noticed one more piece of newspaper tucked in the bottom corner of the trunk. We thought there was nothing in it but soon discovered a tiny shot glass. Roughly etched in the side of the tiny glass was the simple name "Jessie." I removed the glass from the trunk and put it in my kitchen cupboard. Over the years, it was used often for cough syrup or small measurements of food or the kids' "show and tell."

Since its acquisition in 1970, some of the trunk's contents have not survived the test of time. For example, the trunk itself was sold to a local Deejay, and the armadillo shell became a hat modeled by the lady who chose it in a white elephant party. Meanwhile, I became fascinated with Jessie's story and over the years dabbled in piecing it together. Early one wintry morning in 2003, I typed "Eagle, Alaska" into the Internet search engine and from that appearing answer, one lady's incredible life began to take shape. This is the story I want to share. This is Jessie's story.

Alaska Pioneer Home

Sitka, Alaska

Photo by Geoffrey Wyatt

Acknowledgements

Each task of Jessie's story has been a learning experience – gathering, sorting, weeding, deciding, wrestling, tweaking, and turning loose. There are bits of information gleaned from travels, interviews, letters, emails, well-known pieces of literature and little, or unknown, writings. My gratitude runs deep for each and every bit of information shared – especially for patient souls like ...

...Historian Doug Beckstead (U.S. Park Service – Fairbanks) who convinced me that travel in the early 20th century could not happen at today's speeds. He also shared maps, photos, books, etc. educating me about placer mining.

...Carol Knight Copeland, as a child, was Jessie's neighbor. Not only was she a wealth of information and enthusiasm, Carol traveled to my home and shared with me stories and home movies, and gifts from Jessie's trunk.

...Jean Turner and Theresa Dean, curators *extraordinaire* of the vast Eagle, Alaska, museums, have been invaluable sources of information.

...Bob Morton not only shared about meeting Jessie in Rampart in the summer of 1948; he also sent me seven of Jessie's treasured books.

...Nellie, Alberta, Elsie, Stanton Patty, Rosco Pirtle, Dr. Gary Cole, R .N. DeArmond, Chief Isaac of Eagle Village, Sedro-Woolly Museum, and Sherry Foster – some had a thread of information; some had little – but all were enthusiastic helpers.

...Shasta College Instructor and Museum Curator Dottie Smith helped with information about Albert's death, Kennett, California, and Hoopa basketry.

...Local Studies Librarian Sylvia Pybus of Central Library, Sheffield, England

...Alaska State Archivists house a wealth of information about the July Creek Placer Company.

...Individuals I will never meet in this lifetime who had the foresight to document stories they heard of residents of Eagle – particularly Elva Scott and Alsa Gavin.

...My supportive children, who believed in my abilities to write. Daughter Patty who listened to my every doubt or revelation, and designed the cover of the book plus hours of assembling it. Son Geoffrey who read a very early version and was my most honest critic. He also searched for and photographed my many requested photos. Son David who, in spite of a busy life, checked on the book's progress.

...Individual Christians from the Church of Christ who read the manuscript in various stages and encouraged me to "Keep on keeping on."

...Medical staff at Oregon Health Sciences University Parkinson Disease Center who keep me upright and mobile.

...Ron and Joanne Roberts, whose friendship with us has endured years and continents of separation. Now, however, we are blessed to live near each other.

Some Sources of Information

Baranof Banner Newspaper, Sitka, Alaska April 10, 1958. page 9.

Beckstead, Douglas. *The World turned Upside Down: A History of Mining on Coal Creek and Woodchopper Creek Yukon-Charley Rivers National Preserve, Alaska.* U.S Department of the Interior National Park Service. 2000.

DeArmond, R. N. *Tales of a Klondike Newsman.* Mitchell Press Limited. Vancouver, Canada. 1969.

Dickens, Charles. *The Posthumous Papers of the Pickwick Club.* Penguin Books. London. 1836-37.

Gavin, Alsa F. *Walking Among Tall Trees.* Dragon Press, Delta Junction, Alaska. 1991

Garfield, Brian. *The Thousand-Mile War: World War II in Alaska and the Aleutians.* Ballantine Books. New York. 1969.

Graef, Kris Valencia. *The Milepost. All-the-North travel guide.* Morris Communication Co. Updated annually.

Ibsen, Henrik. *A Doll's House: And Two Other Plays*. J. M. Dent & Sons. London. 1914.

McPhee, John. *Coming into the Country.* Noonday Press, New York. 1976.

Mitchell, Ruth. *My Brother Bill: the Life of General "Billy" Mitchell.* Harcourt, Brace and Company. New York. 1953.

Montross, Percy. *Clementine.* Popular song – circa 1880.

Murie, Margaret E. *Two in the Far North.* Alaska Northwest Books. Portland. 1993.

Pyle, Ernie. *Home Country.* Wm. Sloane Associates, Inc. NY. 1935.

Scott, Elva R. *Jewel on the Yukon Eagle City.* Eagle, Alaska. 1997.

Specht, Robert. *Tisha: The History of a young Teacher in the Alaska Wilderness.* Bantam Books. 1977.

Webb, Melody. *Yukon the Last Frontier.* University of Nebraska Press. 1985.

Wickersham, Hon. James. *Old Yukon: Tales – Trails – Trials*. Washington DC Law Book Co. 1938.

CHAPTER 1

I sit in utter darkness. Oh, I am aware that most people know there is little darkness this time of year in the Land of the Midnight Sun. From my room, the only sounds I hear are the muffled blend of the Sitka High School band playing a Sousa march, the Tlingit Indian chants as they dance their way the short distance of the parade route, the piped Russian music aboard the float for the New Archangel dancers, and the children squealing as they race for the saltwater taffy being pitched from the fire trucks. I can picture exactly the activities of the Independence Day parade for I have often participated in this American celebration. However, this year, I prefer the comfort of solitude in my own room surrounded by things that are familiar to me. The year is 1969.

Everything I own is in this little room or stored somewhere in this grand-hotel style building known as the Sitka Pioneer Home. The bed and nightstand were here when I came. On the nightstand are two items – a lamp and a small shot glass. I can feel my name etched in the side of the thin glass and remember well the day and circumstances of this acquisition. The armoire, in which my clothing is kept, is quite old and has served me well. The secretary was my father's own writing desk; its smoky mirror has needed replacing for many years. This was among the items I shipped ahead in 1951 in anticipation of moving immediately to Sitka. My friends

Mr. and Mrs. Knight helped me package and ship two steamer trunks and one wicker trunk – all loaded with life's treasures.

I can still feel the presence of loved ones as I sit in my mother's beautiful chair. It is an elaborate piece of furniture with original japanned finish and delicate pearl inlay on the center back. The fragrance of chrysanthemums reminds me of the recent loss of my good friend John E. Olsen. He was my nearest neighbor in Eagle, close enough that we shared a "two seater" and many laughs. Since my Sitka arrival in 1954, he had been my eyesight when venturing off campus. I had become his mind in more recent years.

I have opened this trunk today and brought out the rough cloth to hold one more time. I close my eyes and hum softly in my now crackling soprano voice "God Save the Queen" and picture children playing on rolling pasturelands. My mother's flag represents all that was once dear to me and reminds me once again of what might have been.

******

"Jessica Jane," Father's American guest dubbed me as he bounced me on his knee. "You will some day marry a prince and be called Lady Jessica." I do not know why or how it came about that, in the year of our Lord 1885, Doctor Henry M. Tichenor had crossed the Atlantic Ocean to be Father's extended guest in our Sheffield, England, manor. I do know that he was neither the first nor the last such guest. However, he was the first in my memory to call me Jessica.

"My name is Jessie Elizabeth Fox! Jane is my *grandmère*! Not me! I am only four years old."

"I know," he whispered. "But, in America, Jessie is an ordinary name; and there is nothing ordinary about you, young lady. Why, there is even a wild-west outlaw who shares your name."

True to Dr. Tichenor's words, Americans have always called me Jessica. I believe it is because of my British accent that they have considered me to be a formal person. I never correct them but for many years, when addressed as Jessica, I thought to myself, *In truth, my name is Jessie.*

I knew at a very young age that many a young girl only dreams of being a part of the world into which I was born. The setting of my birth was a quaint little village near Sheffield, England, in South Yorkshire, during the reign of Queen Victoria. I was born to, and grew up in, a family of substantial wealth. My father was Doctor Walter Caughey Fox, and his father was Doctor William Fox. Together, they owned the Fox Pharmaceutical Company. Many times have I heard Father lament, "I have never felt the need to be practical, for I have never lacked the means to do or to own anything my heart desired."

My father was a large man. Standing beside him, my mother seemed even more petite than she truly was. Mother grew up in Pendleton, Lancaster, England. In my youth, she was usually preoccupied with social duties and teas and calling on other ladies and, of course, receiving callers. Still, fresh in my memory is the fragrance of Mother's perfume as I sat close beside her while she answered my question, "How did you and Father meet?"

"We met on a cruise to Greece. I spotted the most handsome gentleman as he was boarding the ship. He was giving orders to his porters and the purser. I remember thinking how in command of everyone he was. My opinion has never changed."

"Did he see you?" I inquired.

"Oh, he still vows he did not notice me, but I will always believe otherwise. As you know, it would have been highly improper for either of us to have spoken without a formal introduction. I know for certain he saw

3

me on the third day of our journey for the seas were quite tumultuous that day. Many of the passengers were leaning over the railing as though wanting to view each wave on the ship's hull."

"Let me just say I loaned him my handkerchief," Mother would continue. "The next day, the handsome young man persuaded the ship's captain to invite my companion and me to join him for dinner at the captain's table. The evening's invitation was delivered at tea time with my clean handkerchief and a flower. At dinner, the captain graciously introduced everyone at his table.

"The captain said, 'May I present Miss Jessie Helen Rebecca Ellis?'"

"Was that when Father started calling you Your Highness?"

"Yes. When he learned my middle initials were H. R., he immediately told me that it stood for Highness *Royale*. I think he invented that idea, but that is when he started calling me Your Highness."

Mother always ended her story the same. "Thus it was that I, Jessie Helen Rebecca Ellis, met and married the handsome young Doctor Walter Caughey Fox, who became your father. And thus it was that we moved into the Fox family manor in Handsworth, Yorkshire, England. And thus it was that two years later you were born. And two years after your birth, Albert was born. Of course, you know we named him for Queen Victoria's beloved Prince Albert?"

"Yes, I know."

Albert's addition to the family is one of my favorite childhood memories. From the moment I first laid eyes on my little brother, I adored him. He was a happy child, with a reddish tint to his blond hair and fair skinned except for his rosy cheeks and just a hint of devilish twinkle in his eyes. He was perfect in every way…unlike me.

My hair was dark, my complexion nondescript. My worst feature was my eyes. They were the first thing people noticed about me. All my life, I have been aware of stares. At birth, I had no eye pupils; this meant that I was born blind. However, because of my father's contacts in the medical community, a surgeon was located who was able to correct the problem while I was still young. The surgeon slit each eye twice. After surgery, I could see but with quite limited peripheral vision.

I remember well how cousins and visiting children would tease me, "Jessie has the eyes of a cat!" or, when out of range of adult's hearing, they would taunt me with a sing-song "Cat eyes! Cat eyes!" or the dreaded "*Renard!* Fox!" and dodge my attempt to catch them or, worse yet, stand to my side or back where they were out of my limited range of vision. My family never treated me as though I were different from anyone else. As a matter of fact, they encouraged me to be stronger in any situation.

One day, as I was reading aloud to my governess from our family Bible, I came across a lady named Leah. She had tender eyes and, because of that, her younger sister was chosen first to marry. However, her father tricked the groom and substituted Leah for the intended bride. Her husband actually eventually married both sisters. In the end, Leah was the wife who was chosen to be buried in the family plot. I somehow gained encouragement from her story.

******

It is hard for Americans to understand that until I was an adult, I had neither washed nor combed my own hair nor even dressed myself. When our nanny would take "fresh air" walks, she chose to ride the tram into Sheffield city. With Albert in his perambulator and me holding tight to the handle, we would disembark from the trolley at the Town Hall Square and join the throngs of people bustling among those tall, brick structures that to my child's eyes were as big as Nottingham Castle. When it would rain, we would run for cover under the store awnings.

When in public, children spoke only when spoken to. Because our nannies were usually French, most of what we said was *bonjour* and *merci*! We were as comfortable speaking the French language as English. We seldom entered any businesses but rather strolled along while the nanny looked in the windows at varied wares for sale. Of particular fascination to me were the tea stores with their beautiful cups and saucers and china tea pots and the scent of cinnamon and foreign spices wafting through the open doorways. I can still smell the delicate fruity teas and even the wonderful blend of curries. Other than window shopping, the nannies liked to go to the city to meet and greet other nannies.

One such occasion led to a significantly scary moment in my life. While the nannies were exchanging greetings, I became disinterested in the adult conversation going on around me and turned loose of my appointed spot and walked a few steps away to look at my reflection in the spotless glass of the store front. When I realized the conversation around me had stopped, I turned to find that the spot I had left was now empty.

Where are Nanny and Albert? What am I to do? Where could they have gone? Should I stay put or look for a bobby? I had never been alone or lost before, and I began to panic. My heart and finger tips ached from fear. And, then, just as I started to cry, Nanny spoke, "*Qu-avez vous? What is the matter with you?*" And there they were...just steps away from me...but I could not see them because they had moved out of my peripheral vision. That was an important lesson I never forgot in my entire life. *Slow down...take your time to see around you...know your surroundings...don't let others see your fears.*

After the family moved to 32 Crescent Grange in Sheffield, our nanny would walk us to the public gardens where we would sit on benches and watch the parade of lovely ladies seeking *"l'amour."* I was very young to understand the *nuances* of love. I did comprehend that it was entertaining. Everyone seemed in such joyful attire and in circumstances. From eleven in the morning until two in the afternoon, the coy young women stood in or near the gazeboes, pretending animated talk with others like themselves. They would be dressed in pastel gowns of organdy and lace, shading themselves with dainty, matching parasols.

"The ornate handkerchief is perfumed." Nanny once pointed out to me. "Watch how the lady intentionally drops it just in time for a gentleman to pick it up. Then he will ever-so carefully present it to the lady as they gaze into each other's eyes."

I must have been twelve or thirteen years old when Governess Rosalind informed me, "One day you will also meet and fall in love with just such a gentleman." That was an impressionable time in my life. I constantly dreamed of the armored knight who would, one day, whisk me away from whatever doldrums had captured me. I began to think about important matters such as curtsying and pouring tea. About that same time, I started being much more serious about my art and music.

Sometimes, on Sundays, we would visit the gardens as a family. With Father and Mother, we could go into the conservatory.

"Watch this." Albert would say with a wink as we entered the rooms of muggy heat and heavy floral fragrance. "I have found a garter snake (or a frog or a spider) among the plants." He then would manage to frighten some unsuspecting damsel and earn Father's discipline upon our return home.

On Sundays, the ladies' fashions were truly elaborate. I loved to watch the parade of enormous hats that matched, or at least accented, the starched and fitted dotted-swiss or organdy dresses, stockings, and crepe or silk or velvet ribbon sashes.

7

Albert and I each had our own pony by the time I was six years old. Once, when his nanny and my governess were conversing, he and I rode our ponies a little beyond our set limits. Looking skyward, I pointed to a circling bird of prey, and said, "Look, Albert, a vulture. They say when they are circling, they know there is something dead to eat below.

"Do you suppose it thinks we are dead?" he queried. But we quickly decided that we were not its intended dinner. "Jessie, do you think they would eat us if we were lying in the path?"

"I do not know; we could fall off and find out." I giggled.

"Okay. On the count of three, let's fall off and pretend we are dead. One...two.... three..."

We slid to the ground, having failed to consider that it had been raining. We landed in the mud but were determined to lure the creature down. With one eye open, we stayed perfectly still. Eventually, we could hear another horse coming along the path. When the sound of the approaching animal stopped, the rider stepped down and walked over between us. Next, we heard Father's booming laugh as he said, "What are you two doing?" Father enjoyed telling that story for years to come; Mother was not so happy to see her two muddy children. Uncharacteristically, she gave our governess a tongue lashing.

As was customary for wealthy families, Albert was sent to boarding school when he turned eight. I continued my education tutored by my Governess Rosalind, and I missed Albert terribly.

Meanwhile, I was learning important subjects befitting a lady of the time. Early on, I excelled in music...piano, voice, and violin...and later, other stringed instruments. I disliked handwriting and embroidery and art (except flowers), mostly anything that required the extended use of my eyes. Reading was an exception; I have always loved to read.

I lived in an era and region of rich literature. At first, I struggled with Shakespeare but enjoyed seeing his plays performed by such great actors as Martin Harvey. Anything written by the Brontes or Jane Austin was recommended by Queen Victoria herself. If she showed favour for anything, any taboos were lifted. I loved Charles Dickens' writings, including his dark literature; and even *Pepy's Diary* held my interest. But, I digress.

About the time Albert left for boarding school at age eight, Father decided we needed a country home. We soon moved to a suburb of Sheffield. Our residence was Cherrytree Farm, located in the Nether Edge of Yorkshire.

Fox Family Portrait

Photo from Eagle Historical Society

10

CHAPTER 2

"It was erected in 1553." When describing the estate known as Kenwood Glen at Cherrytree, Father always used the term "erected" rather than built because the structure was completely stone. To my memory, the house was enormous, the floors were huge. Peering into the forbidden room from the open doorway, the kitchen was decorated with blue and red, worn tiles.

When I reminisce, I think of trying to see out of the bottle-glass windows. I remember how the dark rooms always felt so cold and damp. Of course, Father still kept the house and all its servants at 32 Grange Crescent for his office and for our town house. Not all of my memories of Cherrytree Farm are pleasant for, even today, I grow melancholy when I think of its splendor. In her Christmas letter dated 1940, Cousin Alice wrote "I am saddened to say that on 12 December, the lovely Cherrytree estate was completely destroyed by bomb in the terrible Sheffield Blitz."

When Albert came home for holiday, he and I would explore the many rooms of the mansion and its every staircase. On one of his visits, Albert and I pocketed some bread from the kitchen staff and decided to explore. We went to the farthest wall from the front entrance to the house. When we reached our destination, we climbed the spiral staircase, sang a child's "eenie, meenie, minie, moe; catch a tiger by the toe" and chose to go left down the long, dark corridor.

When, at last, we thought we had come to the end, we reached out for the wall and found a hidden alcove. Albert carefully brushed away the cobwebs, and we took out our bread and hunkered in the darkness as we nibbled. I thought I felt a spider on my neck. I jumped up, screaming and flailing my arms. Then, I bumped something softer than the stone wall I expected; it seemed to be a rolled up fabric.

"What is this!?" I shouted out amidst all my screams.

"I feel nothing," Albert surmised as he ran his fingers around my head.

"No! Albert! I am fine," I spoke as I calmed. "I had found something." Taking his hand from off my shoulder, I guided him to touch where my other hand rested. The item was very heavy, but the two of us managed to drag it to the staircase and to call out, "Someone help us!" Servants rushed to our rescue and carried the solid roll down the stairs. Once we came to the light of day, we could see that our discovery was a small tapestry of fox hunters. After the piece was beaten clean, Mother had it hung on the library wall.

My clearest memories of Cherrytree are not of the inside but rather the resplendent, multi-colored, fragrant gardens surrounding the manor. Manicured hedge labyrinths led one from floral gardens to herbs and vegetables grown for use by our cook. A field of dainty-leafed cosmos mixed with white and golden daisies bloomed in most seasons. Some of my favorites were pansies, carnations, hyacinth and of course roses. Whenever I could convince Governess Rosalind, I would take my lessons outside. Sometimes, we would sit on a bench near our gardener's cottage for lessons. From memory I once sketched Mother entering this cottage; I am fairly certain that picture is stored in the trunk. I must make a point of searching for it soon. Particularly, the frame is very interesting.

I was naturally curious about the history of the house, but it was completely improper for a refined young lady to muddy her mind with such matters. Mathematics and science were also discouraged. Mostly, I was in training to find a husband, and I was in a good position for that because of my father's wealth. I might even marry a nobleman.

By the time I was twelve years old, I could embroider, sketch, paint (mostly landscapes and flowers), speak French, English, and German fluently, walk with a book on my head, quote the introduction to Chaucer's *Canterbury Tales*, dance the waltz, ride a horse, and know from memory hundreds of "Victorian Don'ts." Among the most important were "Don't let your ankles show...Don't ever put your gloves on in public places...Don't let your dress trail on the ground... Don't show too much of your snowy white neck...when invited to tea, Don't arrive early...Don't wear powder...AND (last, but not least) Don't read novels." It was a strict era. Yet if Queen Victoria seemingly bent the rules, soon everyone felt free to do the same. Fortunately for me, Her Royal Highness had read *Adam Bede* and commissioned a painting depicting its effect on her. Also, the Queen was actually seen publicly tittering at some shocking line in *The Importance of Being Earnest*. By the time I attained the ability to appreciate what I was reading, that prohibition was lifted. Books have always brought me pleasure. Often I have substituted literary friendships for human contact.

I loathed being an only child and longed for Albert's company. When home for holiday, he loved to spend his time outdoors and often asked me along. The only time I can recall Father taking the board to Albert was on just such an occasion. Albert not only knew every square inch of the house, he had explored the grounds surrounding it. He enjoyed explaining to me his treasure hunts, and an occasional treasure find.

"With all of the property including George Wostenholm's elaborate manor at Kenwood Park," Albert said, "there are rumored to be hidden tunnels. Very possibly they were abandoned coal mines." On one of his escapades toward Kenwood Park, Albert happened upon a tunnel. When he hunted me down to share his discovery, his eyes were the only part of him that was not blackened.

"Jessie," he said, "I have found the most incredible thing today. I think that it is an abandoned coal mine, but I am not sure. Some day I will show you, but meanwhile, this is our secret. Could you go fetch me a change of clothes?"

"What are you going to do with those?" Mother inquired of me when she saw me carrying Albert's clothes to my room.

I answered half truthfully, "Albert's pitcher did not have as much water as mine so I told him I would get his clothes if he would like to use my water. You know how he can get when he is playing outdoors."

Albert hid his dirty clothing at a tunnel entrance, where he could change into and out of them every time he wanted to explore. He would often have tales of finding lanterns and coins and bottles and more passageways. Finally, one day he asked if I would like to go with him.

"Oh, yes!" I replied.

That is when he told me what he had learned about his discovery. He said, "I have found an entire network of tunnels and subterranean passageways, and some of them are rumored to even lead to Nottingham Castle and to the market square in Sheffield. It is just so amazing!" When we arrived at the entrance of his find, he lit a candle and placed a chimney over it.

Albert was fascinated by everything in the tunnels, pointing out the moisture on the walls and every outcropping and turn. To me, it was dark, cold, confusing, and scary. At one point, he whispered, "Stay right here. I'll be right back." And off he went, leaving me in total darkness.

It was then that I realized I had never been alone in my entire life. I did not like the feeling of aloneness. *If I ever escape unscathed, I will never allow myself to be alone in this life.*

It seemed an eternity passed before Albert returned to my side. I can still feel the ecstasy of seeing his light coming toward me. When we did approach the tunnel entrance, it was no longer daylight. We could hear distant voices, calling. As we neared the voices, we could decipher they were calling our names. When the seekers saw two filthy ragamuffins, they took us straight to Cherrytree to clean us up and to feed us. Father was waiting at the front door and took Albert straight to the woodshed. I stood outside the door where I witnessed my brother's punishment. I stuck out my tongue at Father although his back was to me, and he was unaware of my presence.

While Albert chose to spend his time grubbing around underground, I found pleasure in the garden. Of course, I was not allowed to plant or harvest fresh food or flowers, but I could paint them or talk to them or arrange them or admire their beauty and fragrance.

By the time I turned eighteen, I was well prepared for any suitors I might have. Mother and I spent hours daily preparing for my "coming out," when I would be introduced to the world. We made trips to London to study ladies' fashion by observing the latest styles and visiting fashion designers and fabric and millinery shoppes. On one journey to London, I found a lovely pattern of Royal Crown Derby china with the exquisite Imari floral patterns in cobalt blue and red and hand painted 24-karat gold. Along with linens and other finery, I placed my first plate in a trunk.

"Look, Albert," I boasted. "I have completed the most exquisite table scarf." I wanted him to see my embroidery and pulled him into the room which held my newly acquired "Hope Chest."

"That is no hope chest," he teased. "They call that a despair barrel. You, Dear sister, are entirely too young to be thinking of such matters."

When I had a free moment, I was practicing elocution and dreaming which royal family I would marry into. I had approached Father with the idea of allowing me to become a nurse and be his helper. That did not set well with him at all.

"Only young ladies whose parents are poor would even consider a career." It was certainly below our station.

With just two days to go before my "coming out," I wanted to model some of my fashionable purchases for Father. When I tried on the special *piece de resistance* (the green dress purchased specifically for the cotillion, the right of passage, the coming-out event), Father asked, "What are the red splotches on your shoulders?" Upon closer examination, it was discovered that I had the chicken pox. The timing of being pocked on the eve of meeting my future husband was devastating. Needless to say, I failed to become a debutante.

The grand ball took place without me. When it was deemed safe, Cousin Alice called on me with flowers, candy, her dance program, and news of who wore what and who met whom. Supposedly, her intention was to cheer me. After my itching stopped and spots disappeared, I pouted in bed for some time and could not even open my beloved books.

After what seemed like several depressing weeks, Father came to my room and suggested I try traveling with Governess Rosalind. Actually, by this time, her title had become more personal maid. We could travel to France or Germany and still be back in time for Cousin Alice's wedding. After giving his idea some serious thought, I began traveling throughout

Europe. Included in my album of postcards collected over years are photos of the Greek Islands, France, Germany, Holland, Italy, Ireland, Scotland and, of course, much of England.

Immediately following Cousin Alice's wedding, Albert came home from Cambridge. He gobbled down his dinner and sat fidgeting, waiting for Father, Mother, and me to finish our meal in customary silence.

"Father." Albert stammered "Mother. I have an opportunity for employment that I wish to discuss with you both."

Father daubed at the corners of his mouth and plopped his serviette on the table, rolling his eyes heavenward. "And just what is so important about this that you could not wait until *après le repas?*"

"Forgive my impatience, Father. Two of my friends are leaving in the morning to reserve passage to America, and I was to meet them an hour ago to tell them if I would join their venture."

"America?" Father boomed. "How can you possibly learn our pharmaceutical business while dilly dallying around the world? We need for you to apprentice here."

"Father." Albert forced his posture and his voice to be respectful. "I have never shown any interest in the family business. My degree is in electrical engineering. I want to work with my hands. There are British companies hiring workers in the California gold mines."

"California? Gold mines?" Father interrupted Albert's plea. "Who will carry on Fox Pharmaceutical? What will your grandfather say? Electricity!" At that, Father exploded, pushed his chair back, causing it to tip over. Paying no attention to the rush of servants to straighten the room, he spoke bluntly. "I forbid this whim. We will discuss it tomorrow after I have made house calls."

Then Father sat down in the newly restored chair and called for tea. When he peered at Mother to pour the beverage, he looked stunned.

We all looked her way and saw tears streaming down her cheeks. She uttered not a sound, served tea to Father and me, looked straight at Albert, rose, and silently departed the room.

I never learned what conversation took place between Father and Mother that night. The next morning, Albert crept into my room and placed a kiss on my forehead.

"What time is it?" I mumbled as I tried to rouse.

"It is still quite early, Dear sister mine."

"Why are you waking me?"

"To tell you 'goodbye.' I am taking with me one satchel of clothes and hoping to meet my friends in Liverpool. Promise me you will write. Promise me you will not allow Father to dictate your life, Dear Jessie."

CHAPTER 3

Some four years later, on the 10th day of June 1908, accompanied by Rosalind, I left England for Kennett, California. The purpose of my journey was to visit Albert. Liverpool was my port of embarkation. My journey from New York's Grand Central Station to Chicago was marred only by the excessive heat. I had read about an Iowan farmer who, in order to protect himself from the sun's fierce rays put up his umbrella, but no sooner was it up than it caught fire. I did not believe the story at the moment of reading, but experiences sometimes change ideas. When I reached Chicago, which might still have been in Iowa as far as heat was concerned, I felt my weight was twice my normal, or so I told my diary.

Here, my passage cost me $5.00, for I enquired of the first train to Denver. There was a special express leaving three hours before the train on which my New York ticket was slated. For the privilege of taking the earlier train, the extra was asked. The conductor was very nice about it, and I thought that the extra time would have passed quietly. But in the short interval between stations, some of the stages in the Purgatories came to mind. A thunderstorm in Nebraska cooled the air and made the run to Denver enjoyable. The remainder of the journey was spent in pleasant conversation with fellow passengers. We did leave the train in Denver for a few days. There, we visited in the home of one of Father's cronies, journeyed to Pike's Peak, and visited the Capitol and museums. I did not care for the exhibits of dead animals. While in Colorado, I purchased a book of photographs titled *Gems of Colorado Scenery.* I came across that book not long ago when rummaging in the trunk; I had completely forgotten I had it. The closer we came to our Sacramento *rendezvous* with Albert, the slower the train seemed to be traveling.

I sat next to the window facing the front of the train, anxiously watching for Albert's familiar face among the throngs of people. The conductor had just walked by calling out "Next stop, Sacramento." It was hard to believe that Rosalind and I had actually braved the Atlantic Ocean from Liverpool to New York and traveled across the entire United States to see my "baby" brother. Now, we were about to visit gold country. Rosalind was fussing over gathering my handbag and hat boxes when I spotted Albert in the mulling crowd.

"Oh! I see his handsome face; right there! By the ticket agent!" I pressed my nose against the window and frantically waved. He spotted me and waved back. He looked thinner than I remembered and, yet, very muscular. It was obvious he was working at manual labor. I wondered what Father would say if he were to see Albert now.

As soon as the train came to a complete stop, I jumped to my feet and joined the crowd trying to escape the oven we had been cooped up in for days. When I took that last step toward the earth, "Sir Galahad Albert" himself perfectly timed reaching out his hand to assist my descent.

Rosalind quickly opened my parasol and handed it to me. The mid-afternoon sun beat down on us as we waited for the next train north.

Fortunately, there was time to purchase a postcard to mail home. The picture was of a statue of Columbus and Queen Isabella displayed in the Rotunda of the State Capitol in Sacramento, California. I addressed the card to Mrs. Fox 32 Grange Crescent, Sharrow Sheffield, England. The message, obviously written in haste (and in pencil) said, "Arrived 4:55 p.m. & Albert was here to meet me."

20

"What joy it is to see you! We have so much catching up to do!" I bubbled.

Trying to be the perfect host, Albert offered, "I have prepared a basket of fresh California fruits and some venison jerky. I'm sorry we do not have tea, but there will be time for that later. Meanwhile, I have brought some jars of spring water from the Shasta fountains. It is supposed to be miraculously healthy. Father would be happy."

While Rosalind took care of gathering the baggage, Albert took me by the arm and shuffled me into the train station. There, he seated me so that he might direct the porter where to set my parcels until we connected with the train that would take us north to Kennett, California. My first impression of my sweet brother was how happy he seemed, and my second impression was how dirty his fingernails were.

Albert was in charge of all arrangements from here. He informed me, "Our train North will not arrive for another two or three hours. There is a park only a stone's throw away. If you are not too tired, we could walk there and try to have a spot of water and pretend it is tea."

"I would like the walk. And the tea."

We sat under an enormous live oak tree that hung low, with its branches far reaching. Albert opened the jar of clear water he had brought from the Shasta fountain. At first, our conversation was formal.

"How are Mother and Father?"

"They are both doing well. They send their love, you know."

"How was your journey?"

"It was a bit tiring in places, but it was a lovely trip." It did not take us long to fall into our childhood banter.

"Along with her love, Mother sent enough tea and delicacies for an army! And, of course, Father sent some healthful herbs and medical advice AND an Ascot tie – the latest fashion."

"Oh, my. I have not even seen a tie in Kennett. I'd be laughed out of town! Perhaps I'll go to San Francisco one day; then I would need a tie. Incidentally, it will be much cooler when we get to the mountains; you won't have to worry about sweating this much."

Rosalind gasped.

"Now, Albert," I said in my most authoritative voice, "Men sweat; women glow!"

"How soon we forget." He beamed as he rolled his eyes skyward.

As the sun was beginning to set, we could hear the train whistle in the distance. Albert gathered the rubble we had created and quickly stuffed it in the basket. Rosalind and I giggled as we tried to run, our clothing sticking to us from the heat, hindering our every move. Albert was trying to be polite and not abandon us. He would run a few steps, then turn to face us as he would take a few steps backwards, calling for us to hurry. Then, as he would start to stumble, he would gain a few steps before turning again to us.

When we arrived at the station, Albert paid the porter to load my enormous trunks and satchels onto the Southern Pacific. Then he seated me on the right side of the train by the window. He said I would not see much in the darkness of night, but any glimpse of the scenery would astound me. Albert was correct predicting that I would miss the scenery. I did feel the first jerk of the train leaving the station, but that was all I remember. I fell asleep sitting upright, for this was a train for laborers and did not have a sleeper car.

Just as I was rousing, the conductor called out "Kennett- next stop!" I looked out of the window and saw that dawn had not quite arrived. My eyes could not quite focus on objects, moving or otherwise; it seemed as though everything had been bathed in grey. Albert stepped down the stairs first, followed by Rosalind, then me. Two of Albert's friends were on the platform. They had come to assist with my baggage so that Albert could get changed into his work clothes. His journey to meet me in Sacramento cost him a day's wages. He had promised his employer not to take any unnecessary time off during our visit.

John and Daniel, Albert's co-workers in the Iron Mountain Mine, placed our baggage on a horse-drawn trailer. They suggested we would be more comfortable walking. Our accommodations were to be in the Kennett Hotel, which sat directly beside the railway tracks. I would take my meals nearby. We walked up a rather steep roadway to a lovely Victorian house built of wood. There was not even a hint of rockwork or brickwork.

As we approached the house, Albert explained, "This is where you will be eating. Mrs. Lorde is a widow. She is probably in the kitchen right now. We will just leave your belongings in the cart. After work, we can help you move everything to the hotel."

"How sweet of you; it would be extremely appreciated. Don't let us keep you from your task."

As soon as they were out of sight, Rosalind and I followed the aroma wafting from places as-yet-to-be explored. In the kitchen, we ran into Mrs. Lorde and introduced ourselves.

Rosalind said she was relieved that I offered her services any time Mrs. Lorde would need them. After all, Rosalind's duties on the journey had been so much simpler than when we were at home. She washed and styled my hair, drew my bath, ironed and set out my clothing for the day, stayed available to dress me—the biggest task there was cinching the corset. She brought me tea and biscuits in the morning, and set up my service for the afternoon tea. I still changed clothing three times daily, compared to six or seven times when at home. She read to me if I so desired, but Rosalind was a slow reader, and I preferred to read silently. And read, I did. Albert worked all daylight hours with very few days off during my stay. And by the time he cleaned up from his work and had a late supper, we might fit in a game of Whist or Hearts or Pedro. He was always so exhausted, I even won a few games.

On September 16th, I wrote Mother the following message on a postcard containing a photo of the United States Fisheries in Baird, California: "We are spending part of a day here and it just pours & Al couldn't get off any other day. Love from Jessie." We had traveled all of one mile from Kennett for this experience.

On my own, I did see a few sights including mining operations and some of the Shasta Springs fountains. The trees and mountains were spectacular sights. I have tried recalling how I came in possession of several baskets woven by Hoopa natives who resided on a reservation near Kennett. I believe one of Albert's friends knew someone who knew someone on the reservation and was able to obtain several baskets, which I took back to England. I gave two to Mother for her Christmas present. Those baskets lie in my trunk, little used.

In mid-November, The Iron Mountain Mine was closed briefly due to heavy snowfall. This meant that Albert had time off. That was our best visit together because we actually had time to talk.

As we sat sipping tea in Mrs. Lorde's parlor, Albert turned to me and blurted, "Well, tell me, Sister Dear. Will you ever marry and collect that dowry?"

"In truth, Brother Mine, there is a touch of romance in my life."

"Mine also. "

"Really! Tell me about her. Do I know her? Is she American? Who is she? When can we meet?"

"Her name is Hannah, and she is in England. She is Daniel's sister; he is my friend who helped me move your things into the hotel. Her parents and she came for a visit, and I have been thinking of little else

24

since we met. She has the most amazing grey-blue eyes. When she looked at me, it was as if she understood what I was trying to say even without my speaking; which is good, because I was terribly tongue tied around her."

"You? Tongue tied! This I would love to see!"

"I want you to get to know her. When you return to England, would you please call on her and deliver a letter on my behalf?"

"You really are serious, aren't you?"

"Oh, yes. More than you will ever know. But, enough about me. Tell me about your mystery man."

"His name is Herbert Barber; everyone calls him Bertie. He is not royalty but he is aristocracy. Handsome, well read, smokes a pipe, loves to hunt. What else would you like to know?"

"Where did you meet him?"

"Father introduced us. Bertie came to Father with a toothache and, as they say 'the rest is history'."

"Somehow, this does not sound like Jane Eyre's Mr. Rochester."

"Oh, at first I was quite taken with him. Now, I am not quite so certain. Apparently, he has trothed his love to many ladies of means but never made it to the altar. Like so many, he is content to court me so long as Father's money does not run low."

I grew pensive and looked Albert square in the face as I confided, "I so longed to be wanted like you want Hannah. But this is not a love match; it is a business arrangement." Then all was silent.

Albert took my hand and said, "Let's change the subject. Remember the woodshed? How much trouble I got into when we visited the tunnel?" And so, as we watched the heavy snowflakes drift to earth and heard the crackling firewood warming the room, we lapsed into comfortable conversation of bygone days and childhood memories.

Within a few days, I began my plans to return to England. I knew that I would be traveling during the social season of Christmas, but I had promised to be home by Christmas Day.

Rosalind began packing, and on November 29, she and I boarded the Southern Pacific train in Kennett for Sacramento. In Sacramento, we switched to the Union Pacific line. On December 3, 1908, I posted the following postcard: "We arrived in New Orleans tonight. A lovely day but cold. Love from us both, Jessie. Just traveled over 2,000 miles in the train in 4 days." Doctor Tichenor had sent his groomsman (I can't think of an American equivalent) to escort us to his home, where we were treated royally in "repayment" of Father's generosity over the years. In New Orleans, we boarded the funny little sternwheeler *the Creole* and traveled up the Mississippi River to Illinois. From there, we rode the train to New York. We left American soil on *The Lusitania*, arriving home in time to celebrate Christmas.

CHAPTER 4

To Father's delight, both of his children married in 1911. Albert was financially able to send for his lovely Hannah. She traveled alone to Kennett, California, to become his bride. One year later, Albert was hired by the Guggenheim and Kennicott Company to work as an electrical engineer for their Canadian operation in Dawson City, Yukon Territory. Albert accepted the employment. As soon as Hannah and baby Walter were able to travel, he moved his little family to Canada.

Since the world was at such unrest, with murmurs of pending war, it would have been improper for me to have an elaborate wedding. Besides, The Honourable Herbert Barber, otherwise known as Bertie, just wanted to set the ceremony of wedding behind us. I wore my cotillion dress as my wedding gown. Cousin Alice was my only attendant. Herbert and I had often talked of Germany for our honeymoon, but that would have been unwise considering the rising international tensions. Instead, we went to the Ascot horse races, an event I had never attended. Father gave Bertie the keys to a cottage for our first home and a sizable dowry. Father also said that Rosalind could continue as my personal maid. A cook and housekeeper came with the residence.

Mother began having health problems of one sort or another. She started speaking of wanting to visit Albert, Hannah, and "Little Walter." In early January 1913, Mother's stepmother had taken ill at home at Chorlton-cum-Hardy in Manchester and passed away. Among the recipients mentioned in her will were her faithful maid Ellen (18 pounds) and the Unitarian Church (50 pounds). Her jewelry and trinkets were left to her only sister Susan Hammond. The Charlton property and whatever wealth remained in the estate after the selling of other properties and the paying of duties were to be divided equally among her late husband's five grandchildren. Albert and I shared in her inheritance with our cousins Florence, Henrietta, and George Carradine. We each were to receive 67.10 pounds cash (American equivalent at the time around $5,000) and one-fifth share of the Charlton property. Father took charge of my portion of the inheritance.

Father thought the timing seemed right for us to take some time together to travel. I do not know for certain whether Samuel Weller was truly the name of Father's groomsman or whether we simply called him that because he reminded us of the Cockney Samuel Weller from *The Pickwick Papers* by Charles Dickens. I rather suspect the latter. But whatever his true name, he was in charge of every detail of the journey. He began by sending Albert a telegram, stating our intentions. Albert wired back that he was pleasantly surprised we would be coming to Dawson.

The note that announced a "family meeting" was posted on our door one morning and discovered by Rosalind as she went outside to polish my shoes. She brought the envelope directly to me. After reading the announcement, I informed Bertie and the staff of our dinner plans. Following a quiet dinner for four with Father and Mother, we adjourned to their library to hear of the plans for our journey.

"Thankee all fer comin'," started Samuel Weller, who then informed us to plan at least one year for traveling. Any place we would be staying for a week or more, he would plan to set up as comfortably as our homes. Mother and I began by requesting certain staff members to accompany us on our expected .excursion. Of course, Father's Samuel Weller and Rosalind and Mother's handmaiden as well as a cook would be the bare minimum to travel comfortably.

Once the staffing was determined, Mother and I began gathering for packing essentials for the journey. We had months to prepare, leaving nothing to chance. We began by thinking of linens to take—for sleeping, bathing, eating, entertaining, and tea time. We needed our own china, which meant tea services, cups, saucers, dishes, bowls, and the all-essential egg cup. This necessitated taking a china closet, our own silver service, a French crystal clock, Father's desk, and Mother's favorite chair. Of course, books and bookcases and a goodly supply of foods were also packed. I decided to take some of the Hoopa baskets, thinking they might be useful when entertaining.

Even though we knew Canada was under British rule, we could not be certain that we would be able to find our favorite teas, biscuits, almond paste, sugars, scones, marzipan, etcetera. We each supervised our personal servant as they packed our treasures. The clothing was of great importance as we kept in mind that many months of our journey would be spent in the Yukon Territory and the wild country of Alaska.

Grandmere's will was read in Manchester on February 11th, and our ship departed from Liverpool February 21st in the year of our Lord 1913. Father, Mother, Bertie, and I were accompanied by three servants and a cook. It was a comfortable crossing. Father and I played card games; Mother and I embroidered and read. Bertie seemed to be constantly occupied with games of chance or visiting. Once on dry land, we took the same route Rosalind and I had traveled, five years earlier, from New York as far as Denver then changed trains to travel north to Seattle.

As we waited in Seattle for our northern passage, we all enjoyed watching the transport of ships through the Lockes. Mother and I took much pleasure in shopping. While the men sought out stores to purchase fishing and hunting attire, we ladies found quaint little mercantiles one would never have dreamed of in England. On the day before our northern departure, we returned to *Ye Olde Curiosity Shop* to make what we deemed a most practical purchase — an armadillo-shell basket. It could be used as a centerpiece for fruit or flowers or even placed on a table by our door to receive cards of callers. That practically unused shell still lies somewhere in my trunk here in Sitka.

Boarding the *SS Princess Patricia* in Seattle, our cruise up the Inside Passage was quite pleasurable. Our British party of seven had changed only slightly, having lost the original cook but acquiring in her place a fine chef. In Juneau, we were able to go ashore long enough to visit and to purchase postcards and to regain our land legs a little. It would take forty years before my feet would touch this part of God's earth again.

Finally, our entourage disembarked in Skagway, where Samuel Weller made arrangements for our passage on the White Pass and Yukon Railroad. When the train paralleled the Chilkoot Pass trail, I was appalled at the number of usable items the gold rushers had abandoned some fifteen to twenty years earlier. Once in Whitehorse, we left the train and Samuel Weller secured our passage on the sternwheeler to Dawson City. It had been a long, arduous journey. I found myself counting down the days and moments it would take to see Albert and his family.

Father had wired Albert from Seattle, giving an estimation of when we expected to arrive in Dawson City, Yukon Territory. His estimation was off by several days, and Samuel Weller had to hunt for Hannah while everyone else sat on crates at the dock, waiting for word. Hours passed. Finally, a buck wagon arrived to gather our belongings. Hannah sent word for us to follow the wagon to their residence. And, follow we did. On foot! Father was appalled.

Once Albert gets home, all will be well. I assured myself. Indeed, it was so good to see my little brother. Albert looked content and so mature. Hannah greeted us affectionately but was obviously unaccustomed to being hostess to visitors. Baby Walter was the spitting image of his father in looks. He must have been cutting teeth for his temperament was very vocal when anyone besides his mother would approach.

Dawson City, in its heyday, was the heart of the Klondike rush for gold. It was the destination of thousands of seekers of gold. There are actual photographs of people heading for Dawson, climbing the Chilkoot Pass carrying everything imaginable – even an upright piano – on their backs. Other than gold, gambling seemed to be the main entertainment at the time of our visit.

In mid-June 1913, our entire entourage boarded the sternwheeler *Yukon* in Dawson City, Yukon Territory, planning to be in Circle, Alaska, in a few days. We all said our tearful "Goodbyes" to Albert, Little Walter, and expectant Hannah as we boarded the steamboat *Yukon*. We were headed north, down the Yukon River.

Russians gave it names like *Juna* or *Jukchana* while Natives have called it *Kuikpak* or *Youcon*. Most people know it as the Yukon River. No matter what it is called, all the names mean the same—"big river." It is indeed a very big river—larger than any in all of Europe. Beginning in Canada, it meanders across the entire width of the State of Alaska; I am told the River is over 2,000 miles long. It looks muddy, but I am told that it is glacial silt that gives it the murky gray appearance. Although the Yukon is long, my first impression of its enormity was less than memorable.

In my life, I have traveled many waterways. In Europe, there were leisurely Sunday afternoons spent in a row boat on a pond. There were journeys of touring Europe in punts and gondolas on such rivers as the Danube and the Thames. There were, of course, ocean cruises. However, stepping foot onto that sternwheeler that day in June 1913 would prove more life changing than anyone could imagine.

We expected to be passengers for several days, getting to Circle, Alaska. From there, we would travel to Fairbanks. From Fairbanks, Father had announced that our party would head south and we should be able to be in Victoria, British Columbia, before November.

That river journey was steady and, for the most part, uneventful. The scenery was mostly black spruce and stands of birch and, of course, water. There were occasional sightings of bears, wolf packs, and porcupine as well as birds such as ptarmigan, swans, and eagles. Without asking Father to check his watch for the time, there was little way to know the hour other than hunger pangs. Meals on the boat were served at all hours because of the constant daylight. What seemed like every few hours, the boat would stop to load wood, necessary fuel for the *Yukon*.

Most of the woodchoppers resided, during the months of thaw, alongside the River in lean-to cabins, although some had created lovely homes in charming settings. They gathered wood and stacked it to feed the large vessels for power. Logs were of uniform size—small around and probably a meter long—enough wood to fill a good-sized parlor. It is said that the woodchoppers became wealthier than the gold rushers of 1898-99. After the wood was loaded, our journey continued.

Onboard, because of the constant daylight Father, Bertie, and I stayed up all night playing cards. We were expecting it would be several weeks before we experienced darkness. Even then, people called the territory the "Land of the Midnight Sun."

I was intent on my embroidery, seldom looking up. Father and Bertie were involved in a game of chance. Mother had gone to her sleeping berth. She usually took a little while to adjust to the boat's motion then she would be fine for the remainder of our journey, or so I thought. When the second bell rang for tea and Mother still had not come, I went to rouse her. She opened her eyes but did not move.

"Bring your Father," she said. "I am quite ill."

"What shall I tell him? Do you need a chamber pot? Or is it something more serious?" She did not answer.

Father came immediately and knelt beside her berth.

"Tell me where you hurt, Your Highness." He was always so tender with her. And he seemed more gentle than ever as he poked and prodded for tenderness. Whatever her malady, it had come on suddenly and violently for she was doubled over in pain.

He sent his trusted groomsman to beckon the vessel's captain.

"How far are we from the nearest medical aide?" Father asked.

"We have one more stop to load wood for feeding this hog. Barring any delays, we should be able to reach Eagle City by morning. When most of the miners left the Eagle City area chasing the gold rush to Nome, some did not leave. There remains an army fort, and the army physician stayed, still awaiting his orders to return stateside." We were relieved to learn that Eagle City also had a telegraph and wireless station.

When the *Yukon* stopped to load wood, it seemed it took a very long time to dock and load the logs necessary to continue. Father felt sure we were going to lose Mother. Though she was often ill, she was not one to complain. Perhaps she had eaten something that did not agree with her. Perhaps it was ague. Time was of the essence to get her to a physician to diagnose her problem. Father stayed by Mother's side. I, being somewhat frantic, positioned myself so that I could see when we might be approaching civilization.

"How will we know when we near Eagle? Are there any landmarks for which to watch?" I inquired of the Captain.

"When we pass Eagle Village, we will still have three miles to travel to reach Eagle City. From the Village, you will glimpse a large rock sloping into the river."

"Is that why there is an army fort in the vicinity?"

"Not exactly. Granted, Fort Egbert was established to prevent war between the gold miners and the nearby tribe, but also to prevent vigilante takeover of Eagle. Only someone who has been an eye-witness of the corruption Soapy Smith and his gang caused in Skagway would understand. Once the American government realized that the Han tribe was not only peace-loving but not at all interested in gold, it was too late."

As we approached a vantage point from which we could see the huge rock well ahead, I pointed to the shore where children were playing around a church. I inquired, "What town is that?"

"That is Eagle Village where a large community of Han Kutchen Athabaskan Indians reside. The community is more populated than Eagle City. They have their own church and school."

The date of our arrival in Eagle, Alaska, was June 22, 1913. I had not even thought about our arrival being on a Sunday or how accessible a doctor might be. Samuel Weller had, however, remembered that we would have to look up the United States Customs officer before we could conduct any business. Looking back, I discovered this was the summer solstice, and I had been awake all night.

Sternwheelers on the Yukon River

Photo from Jessie's Trunk

Eagle's Nest, Killarney, Ireland
Postcard from Jessie's Postcard Collection

Eagle Bluff, Eagle, Alaska
Photo by Betty Wyatt

CHAPTER 5

As we neared the enormous rock known as Eagle's Bluff, I became overwhelmed with emotion. The very first time I laid eyes on it, I thought to myself, *I must be dreaming. Am I back in Killarney? Or am I truly in Alaskan waters?* In all the emotion and confusion of the moment, the sight before me was indeed the very sight of a journey long ago and far away – the magnificent Eagle's Nest Mountain in Killarney, Ireland! At that very moment, I felt at ease about the unscheduled stop.

Once the *Yukon* was docked, the passengers were the first to leave the vessel. I waited to accompany my parents when they disembarked. Mother was so delicate and tiny that one man was able to carry her. When I stepped onto the ramp, I was wishing someone could carry me. From memory, I would say the boards probably had been moved to the Yukon from an abandoned mining claim. Two or three boards had been placed side-by-side over a steep, yet rocky, embankment in an attempt to make a ramp. End-to-end, the twenty feet of boards lacked about ten feet of reaching level ground. When the boards ran out, there were still another several feet to maneuver over numerous sizable rocks. Trust me, my fashionable shoes were not fashioned for this climb.

Ulysses G. Myers was the first person we met when our entire group left the sternwheeler. He was short in stature with a ruddy complexion. One could see that the original color of his thinning hair had been red. He looked up from his desk in the Courthouse, where he was at work, trying to make sense of the bookwork he had inherited from someone who had decided to follow many others in the gold rush to Nome. He stayed seated as each person in our party came through the open door until Father entered the room, and then he stood. I don't know whether he was impressed with Father's size or his suit and tie, but whichever it was, he was ready with answers. His glasses were propped on the end of his nose, but when Father came in, he removed his glasses and set them on the ledger before him. At that moment, he was at his job as Deputy Commissioner, but he quickly set aside the bookwork and spoke to the travelers.

"Do you need the customs officer?" When everyone nodded, Customs Agent Myers lodged the glasses once again on the tip of his nose and placed the book on the bookshelf behind him; asking the strangers if we had anything to declare.

"Well," Father said, with a feeble and inappropriate attempt at humor "I declare it is a warm day, and I declare that my wife is very ill and in need of a doctor and perhaps a hospital."

"Well, we do have a physician. But, with those accents giving you away, I insist on seeing your identification. I am acting United States Customs Officer Myers," he stated firmly as he thrust his hand to shake hands with Father.

"You, too, have an accent. From where did you come?"

"I was sent here by the United States Weather Bureau from Pennsylvania in 1899." He added, "When Fort Egbert was closed down, I let my wife have that job while I began a personal quest for gold. Why don't you have your wife lie on the sofa? I'll get someone to fetch the doctor."

Father helped Mother to the chesterfield, or what the Americans call "sofa."

I stayed by Mother's side while the others in our party filed out onto the road.

Before Father could rise, Mr. Myers had offered us bedding for the night. But Father said we needed nothing. And, indeed, we felt totally prepared for anything life could hand us. When the physician arrived, he listened to Mother's chest and looked down her mouth and ears and took her pulse. I recognized that she had a temperature but beyond that I could not say with certainty what her ailment was. I thought to myself, *Can one get malaria this far north*? Father was trying to comfort Mother as best he could with the remainder of our party standing just outside the door.

Finally, the doctor spoke, "I am afraid that she is very weak and should not be moved for at least a month. She especially should not travel anywhere until her health is improved." It was time for a family meeting. There was never a definitive diagnosis of Mother's ailment; "apoplexy" might be considered a stroke in more modern times. We could leave Mother and her maid and meet up later in Seattle.

Bertie had seemed disinterested up to this point. While Father and Samuel Weller discussed possible solutions, Bertie declared he would get bored, and perhaps he should return to the boat and go back to Dawson. When the next sternwheeler came upriver several days later, that is exactly what my husband chose to do. As soon as his boat departed from Eagle, Rosalind mentioned she had seen our cook onboard with him. Father was particularly frantic at this news. At the time, I thought his reaction was because of the cook disappearing with Bertie, but later I learned it was because of the handsome dowry he had given Bertie upon our marriage.

It took our group a few days to reassemble. Samuel Weller could be located either fishing or imbibing with the locals. I believe Rosalind and Mother's maid found shelter in a vacated army structure.

When they realized that we remaining six would be in town for a month, Mr. and Mrs. Myers said there was a large cabin on the riverfront that would be empty until the owner moved back into town after the first freeze. Mr. Smith, the owner, was a gold miner who had chosen to stay put in Eagle rather than follow the rush to Nome. Of course, we planned to be "long gone" by winter. The Myers felt sure that Mr. Smith would not mind if we used the place in his absence. Perhaps we could pay some rent for it. Father asked Samuel Weller to arrange a nurse for Mother and a replacement cook, which he did immediately.

With Mother resting peacefully, I felt burdensome each time I turned a page or made any sound. Determined not to add to the nurse's duties, I decided to explore the great hamlet of Eagle. Eagle City is not complicated except it is located on a winding, turning area of the Yukon River.

One would think that having lived in the same location for over 40 years, I should have learned which way is North or South or East or West. I have concluded that this was not possible for me because the river flows catawampus. Oh, I know that the sun comes up in the East and goes down in the West. But, when the sun goes down in mid-November and does not reappear until mid-January, that is confusing enough. And when the springtime sun does not rise and set where the autumnal sun does, it is all very confusing.

Not confusing, however, is the layout of the town. It sits today much the same as it was laid out in 1897, before the gold rush had even hit that far north. Judge Wickersham's courthouse and the wellhouse still stand in city center. Redmen Hall and the Fort Egbert mule barn are unchanged. The hospital has been taken down from where it sat in the Fort area, and the church's adjacent rectory burned years ago. Mission Creek still runs beside Eagle Bluff. Two cemeteries continue to receive the bodies of those who have passed on. It did not take me long at all to explore the territory.

If there is any story one would hear when visiting Eagle, it is the wonderful story of Roald Amundsen's visit while searching for the Northwest Passage. In August 1905, he left his ship and crew of six, frozen in ice for the third year, and joined Eskimos traveling south by dog sled to Fort Yukon. He was in need of medical advice for one of his crew who was ill. At Fort Yukon, he learned the nearest telegraph office was in Eagle, Alaska, another 200 miles along the Yukon River. He followed the frozen river, arriving in Eagle on December 4. The temperature was 60° below zero the day he entered town. Arriving broke and shabby, the locals just assumed he was another prospector, down on his luck. Finally, he convinced them of his importance so they would allow him to send a telegram to his home without paying. That telegram was 3,000 words, and because of the cold weather, the telegraph line kept breaking. It took several weeks to get word back from his family in Norway and to receive money enough to continue his voyage. His stay in Eagle was two months, during which time he fit right into the community. The money and good news of home came, and he was able to leave Eagle replenished with supplies and a new dog team and sled for travel to his ship which was 1,000 miles northeast.

Of course, our troop did not look bedraggled when we arrived nor was the river frozen over, but the reception we received on arrival and during Mother's recovery was every bit as warm as that of the great explorer. Mother eventually began to feel strong enough to take short walks along the road by the river front. So long as one would stay on the roadway or beaten paths along the river, it was safe. A fair warning would certainly be to avoid getting too close to the river's edge.

On July 4th, the prospectors came out of the woods in droves. We had no idea the population of Eagle was so great! The people from Eagle Village also came for the American celebration of Independence Day. We, as British citizens, kept a low profile for the day but still enjoyed the festivities which included American flag waving, a parade, a picnic, music and dancing. Contests such as log rolling, tobacco spitting, foot races, and greased-pole climbing were topped off at the day's end by a contest of noisemaking – guns, rifles, banging pie tins, drums, and yelling. It was all in fun. However, Mother insisted I unpack the flag of our homeland for her to hold in secret.

Father had been invited to join in the frivolities of the two local social clubs, Camp Eagle No.13 Arctic Brotherhood and the Improved Order of Redmen Chetuthutlie Lodge No. 6. He enjoyed sharing his cigars and stories, true or not. And he was known to imbibe in occasional drinks.

Somehow he did not quite fit in with the Lodge group, though truth be told, the rosters for both organizations included most of the same men. The Redmen Lodge was started in Boston in 1773 as a result of "The Boston Tea Party." Every two weeks, everyone in town was invited to socialize, which often included card games or dancing. The Arctic Brotherhood allowed cigars and liquor and often included dances or dramatic productions for the entire community.

The doctor had strongly advised Mother against ocean travel. As she became stronger, we started talking about whether or not to continue our journey as originally planned or head south and board whatever ship we might find heading homeward. Meanwhile, Father sent a telegram to his banker in England requesting money be sent by wire to continue our journey.

It took several days for a reply from England. Normally, if Father was worried about something, he did not share his troubles with Mother or me. Nothing in life had ever prepared us for the response Father received in that reply. I will never forget the look in his eyes when he returned with the telegram. He read it aloud to Mother and me. "Doctor Fox. Apparently you have not received word that England is now part of the Great War. Money is inaccessible. Wish I could help, but entire nation is affected. James Hughes, Bank President."

Egg Cups from Jessie's Trunk

Photo by Rosco Pirtle

CHAPTER 6

Now, I must say before I go much further that I have never been one to cry easily. I could probably count on one hand the times in my life I have really cried—the tunnel incident when Albert left me alone in the dark, when Mother's mother died, when Rosalind announced her resignation…well, maybe it would take two hands to count my cries. But, believe you me, the news from England was one of those times. I tried very hard to hide my emotions so that I was not an added burden to Father. However, nothing could stop the floodgates of tears that came. Buckets of tears and hallways of wailing; I was not alone in my misery. I am certain the citizens of Eagle thought us completely mad. Father sent a few more telegrams to friends and relatives and even his barrister, but to no avail. The answer from every source remained the same – funds inaccessible.

Father did still have some money left and announced that he intended to be frugal with his spending. I don't believe he had an inkling of what the word frugal meant.

By mid-August, the town's people were beginning to prepare for winter—gathering wood, stacking it close to (or inside) their houses. Whenever there was any social event (church or whatever) the women had their knitting and crocheting with them, working on mittens and socks and hats and silly nose warmers. I felt secure that we had certainly packed enough layers of clothing and hand- and ear muffs. Father, Mother, and I had even packed our fur coats. We surely were ready.

What I had not anticipated was that our servants would want to return to England, and with a salary. Father always said he was never practical when it came to money. I had never been allowed to muddy my thinking with learning much more than basic addition or subtraction. The staff came together to Father and asked for their passage home, which he granted. I saw him hand them their tickets to England and a cash bonus. His wad of bills was smaller than I had ever seen it. *If only I'd had the gumption to request my passage also.*

The majority of houses in Eagle are made of logs, insulated with moss. Many are structured as shotgun houses, constructed with a front door and a back door. One can stand at either door, point a shotgun; and, as long as both doors are standing open and one's aim is good, any fired ammunition can go directly through the house and out the other door. I have never personally tested this theory. Ed Biederman's place was a shotgun house.

Father's big riverfront house was two stories. One would go in through the front door, entering first the living quarter and a dining area; the next room was the kitchen. To the side of the dining area, one could climb a narrow, steep stairway to the two bedrooms. The *toilette* was out the back door and down the path about thirty feet away.

One morning in late September, I woke to a silent household. The floor was so cold I jumped back into bed and searched for my warming brick, which was almost as cold as the floor. "I must remember today to search for warm stockings. I can't bear the thought of waking to this cold every day." I said aloud. But I was the only listener in the room or even in the house.

I cried silently as I began to realize my breakfast had not been delivered. I covered my head and went back to sleep knowing somehow "This, too, shall pass." But when I woke again, nothing had changed except I could hear Mother stirring somewhere in the house. After what seemed hours, I picked up my stockings and slowly tugged them on, causing a hole in my first attempt. "I must learn to be more careful or my things will never last." Then each shoe, stiff from the cold air, slipped on with great discomfort. "Who will button my shoes for me?" As that question passed my lips, it reminded me of the folk song, "He's Gone Away." In spite of my misery, I found myself humming the questions "Who will tie my shoes and who will comb my pretty hair when he's gone?" My singing did not cheer me, but it did take my mind off my total misery. At that moment, I was concentrating on buttoning my dress in the back without a corset. I will admit before I succeeded getting dressed for that day, I threw the clothes on the floor several times, only to be reminded tantrums would get me nowhere. The person who had to pick them up was none other than myself. I must have looked a mess! The dress would simply not button at the waist, I dared not touch my hair for fear it would never go back into any resemblance of a curl, and the shoes were only partially buttoned. I just hoped there would be no callers today.

When, after what seemed like hours, I emerged downstairs, I found Mother wrapped in blankets sitting by the front window with a cup of tea and some toast.

"Where did you get warm toast?" I squealed.

She pointed to the kitchen, and I realized the local cook from Eagle Village was still with us. I rushed to the kitchen and pointed to the egg cup and bread, indicating that was my order for the morning, and poured myself a cup of tea. I added milk and sugar to my tea and thought to myself, "We should be able to survive this." At that point, I realized the kitchen was toasty warm and moved a chair from the dining area to the kitchen, where I spent the rest of the morning staring out the tiny window at the first snowflakes. It was mesmerizing. This, of course, would not be my last such viewing.

While we still had a cook, and while I was spending so much time in the warm kitchen, I tried visiting with her. At first, it was difficult because neither of us spoke the "American English" language. However, with time and patience, we figured out that we both had the name Elizabeth and that I knew absolutely nothing about survival.

After three days of repeated activity, I realized we might survive the bitter cold, but we needed to learn to live. Father stayed warm and filled by visiting with the men from the Lodge, timing his visits at mealtime. But Mother was too weak to walk on rough footpaths in the snow. Let me say right here that the people from the community and from Fort Egbert were generous particularly with food, but I don't think they realized that we were eating the food they sent at whatever temperature it arrived—usually quite cold.

Building a fire in the fireplace was a lesson unto itself. With outdoor temperatures dipping below minus fifty degrees, I awoke every morning able to see my breath. I felt prepared to tackle building a fire, having studied Elizabeth's fire-building methods—with one addition—I dug through two or three trunks until I found my collection of gloves. From this array, I selected a black kit leather and carefully massaged each finger into place. I felt I needed the gloves to protect me from getting splinters.

Next, I gathered all of the essentials I had noted Elizabeth using— moss, kindling, logs, matches —setting them near the hearth as though I were about to perform surgery. I then placed a split log against the back wall of the fireplace and placed a generous cushion of moss in front of the log. So far, everything seemed to be going smoothly. I crisscrossed pieces of kindling and stacked two logs atop the kindling. Everything appeared to be just as Elizabeth had done.

Finally, I removed my gloves, and struck a match. *Will it light the cold moss? Voila!* Indeed, it did. I felt rather smug about teaching myself the art of fire building without any assistance. My smugness lasted less than one minute. Almost instantly, the room became filled with smoke. I ran to open the doors and windows only to find most of them were frozen closed. I took a cupful of water and tried to douse the fire but that only worsened the thickness of the smoke. Giving no heed to the nightgown I was wearing, I ran out the front door screaming for help.

Mr. Biederman was in the vicinity and heard my cries. After making certain no one was trapped in the fire, he bravely entered the house. Coughing and hacking and waving his arms, he was only inside a moment or two.

"Why was the damper closed?" he asked.

"What is a damper?" I responded.

The rest of the day was spent cleaning everything. As it turned out, it was a lesson well learned just not in a conventional manner. There was plenty more to learn about fires and fire starting and, I might add, fire prevention. I bet there are still people in Eagle talking about the *cheechako* and her ignorant ways.

The other major problem was running water. The local joke is that its "Running water, thy name is woman." The simple reason for this terminology was that the responsibility usually fell on the women to make certain the household had water from whatever source. During warmer climate, the community wellhouse provided water for anyone willing to tote it. Wheelbarrows and wagons come in handy when trying to transport without spilling. Of course, when the snow is deep enough, one does not have to go as far for water, but it takes a lot of snow to melt down to one pan full. Rain is the best source and the best water. Rain water is especially good for washing hair.

We had brought from England a goodly supply of powders, soaps for our bodies and perfumes. One thing I learned early on was "waste not; want not" when it came to conserving water and energy. Fresh water was used for drinking or personal cleanliness or preparing meals, then dishes, then reused to wash clothing or furniture or floors, then pitched onto the garden. Nary a drop was wasted. Baths were infrequent and had to be planned for well in advance.

About the time I learned to boil water on the wood-burning kitchen stove, Mr. Smith, the house owner returned from prospecting. He was very nice about us taking over his residence. He moved into a small cabin next door more as a boarder than a landlord. He remained a good neighbor for many years.

The very first thing I learned to cook was soft boiled eggs for our egg cups. First, one must get the eggs. That is the hardest part. I still chuckle when I recall a letter written from Fort Egbert in 1906. Sergeant Woodfill explained that "When they brought the first chickens in, it was summer. Because it was light all the time, the roosters never knew when to stop crowing and the hens never knew when to stop laying. So they wore themselves out and all died. They solved the problem by building a big chicken house, lit by lanterns. During the summer they chased 'em in there and darkened the windows for 12 hours out of each 24 hours. During the long winter nights they simply lit the lanterns half the time."

And, indeed, our first eggs were a gift from one of the Fort Egbert wives. To perfectly prepare a soft-boiled egg, one covers the egg in cold water and places the pan on the stove; when the water begins to boil, leave it on the stove, boiling, exactly three minutes then transfer the egg to the egg cup; I think I had never tasted anything so scrumptious as my first egg! And I made it myself! Making bread would take a lot more learning.

Meanwhile, Father was getting acquainted with folks from the community. I will never forget the night he invited a gentleman to our table. Father had said there would be a guest for supper so I had added extra water to stretch the broth and prepared some Indian fried bread. I had washed and ironed our finest linens and located the last marzipan in preparation for our first real company. I had even removed our laundry which was draped on every piece of furniture around the house for drying.

Father answered the rapping at the door and invited our guest inside. I actually heard an audible murmur from Mother's corner of the room when, in the dim candlelight, we made out the figure of a very thin, very tall man. Father introduced him to us simply as his friend, Mr. Nimrod. He looked starved, but he was extremely polite for an American. He asked if he could say a blessing for the food before we ate. He talked a great deal about his dream of building a flying machine even though he knew Orville and Wilbur Wright had already made one. He prospected some for gold in the summer, but he preferred to hunt, trap, and fish. As it turned out, "Nimrod" was a name of a great hunter from the Bible and was simply his nickname. It was the first time in my life to speak to a gentleman using other than his surname.

He asked Father if he could see the clock, and Father left the room, returning with our French crystal clock we had brought from home. One could tell that Mr. Nimrod had handled clocks before because he handled it carefully and yet knew which parts could be moved and touched, pointed to problem areas he spotted and knew the names of all its parts. Finally, he told Father he could get it running again for $3.00. Father allowed him to take it. I wondered to myself if there was $3.00 in the house, but I dared not say anything.

After our guest left, Father told me he had heard an unbelievable story about Mr. Nimrod. Father claimed that Nimrod once killed a bear, fashioned for himself a set of teeth from the bear's teeth, and ate the bear with his new false teeth. I was not sure I believed such a tall tale.

Arctic Brotherhood Cup and Plate
From Jessie's Trunk
Photo by Rosco Pirtle

CHAPTER 7

Right away, it became obvious that I would be the family member to take on menial tasks. Looking back, it seems too mammoth a responsibility to face, because each day was a new challenge—water and wood supplies, laundry, light to see by, warmth, fires going, meals and tea time…even personal hygiene took some learning.

Take, for instance, laundry. Often Mother would bring a chair, place it in a kitchen corner, and keep me company. Fortunately for me, when the maids left, they did not take with them the soap. Later, I would have to learn to make my own lye soap. We were very careful not to soil articles of clothing. More importantly, we did not carelessly choose to wash everything. My dear friend Mrs. Knight used to say, "Wood smoke makes a very good deodorant."

The task of laundry would begin by building the fire and heating the oval shaped, copper boiler filled with precious rainwater…. or snow. This was a major job. I would gather snow in a small pan, carry it to the stove, empty it into the oblong boiler and pack it as tightly as possible. In the early days, a quart jar of snow would yield perhaps half of a cup of water. Later, as I grew stronger and less timid, I could almost double that yield. Then, while the water reached the boiling point, I would whittle the lye soap, being careful not to waste any. To make starch, I stirred flour (or for Father's shirts, sugar) into cool water until smooth then thinned down the mixture with boiling water.

If there were dirty spots, I rubbed them on the scrub board. The next step in the washing process was to put the article in the boiling water and push it down with the broom handle, checking as carefully as possible, in the dim light, for soiled areas. Finally, the article was removed from the kettle with a broom stick handle, then rinsed and starched. Again, at first, I was not very strong to wring the cloth, but I learned rather quickly that the more moisture I could get out, the less time it took to dry. Drying clothing in winter was always a challenge; I tried many methods including one horrible failure.

This particular Monday, the outside temperature was 60° below zero and I was out of patience and room for hanging the last little bit of laundry. The moon was full and, once outside, the snow was deep enough that I could drape the towel over the edge of the roof. I took the tea towel outside, left it only a moment, picked the frozen article up by the corners, dashed back inside, waved it up and down twice, and "snap!" the ice fell to the kitchen floor along with pieces of fabric. It was dry! Though tattered! There was no time to cry over this favorite piece of embroidery for I had a kitchen to mop up. Much of the laundry then had to be ironed. That was another day's work. Ironing was a task that took plenty of learning.

I set aside each day of the week for one major task. Monday – "running water," washing; Tuesday – ironing; Wednesday – mending; Thursday – inventory, gardening; Friday – cleaning, dusting, polishing; Saturday – baking; Sunday – church.

Neither Mother nor I had ventured into any social activities since coming to Eagle. One Monday afternoon, Father handed me an invitation to the Camp Eagle No. 13 Arctic Brotherhood Saint Patrick's Day Grand

Ball and Concert to be held March 17, 1914. "Wear green attire" was the only handwriting on the paper.

"Green." I mused, "I can find something green." I had trunks of clothing, and green was one of my favorite colors.

First, I helped Mother select a white blouse with an Irish lace collar and her black skirt. Her choice of green was a brooch with hand painted flowers.

After trying to get into some of my dresses, I finally selected a light green chiffon over embroidered silk. I had never worn it because the waistline was never fitted properly. In this instance, however, that was to my advantage because I had not been wearing a corset and my body had shifted substantially.

When I had finished my tasks on Saint Patrick's Day, and after tea time, I set to work getting dressed for the evening. Water was especially harsh on my hands. No question about it – I would have to wear gloves. I could get my feet into the everyday shoes I'd been wearing for work. The problem of selecting the shoes settled itself. But what was I to do about my hair? I am ashamed to admit that I had neither washed nor combed it since the maids left some months earlier. I just kept tucking the loose strands out of my way and sticking hairpins in to keep it out of my eyes. I dared not take it down at this late time, having not a clue of how to manage it. Finally, as mother was calling for my assistance, I gave up on my hair and chose a very large hat to cover the problem. Anchoring the hat in place with every hat pin I could find (probably six or eight), I rushed out of my room.

Father looked absolutely dashing in his formal attire. Mother took his offered arm, and I followed closely behind. The Arctic Brotherhood Lodge building was located at the corner of Third and Berry at the entrance to Fort Egbert. It was not a distant walk from our place of residence, but it was not easy maneuvering in ice and snow. When we did arrive, I was pleasantly surprised by the number of people who were there, and how formally dressed they were. I, of course, was the only one with a hat. As soon as we were admitted into the great room, Mrs. Myers rushed to my side and handed me a dance program.

"I hope you don't mind, but I allowed some of the earlier gentlemen to sign your card for waltzes. I did not know for sure if you would be acquainted with any other steps. And, then, she very thoughtfully told me the list of dances. "Waltz, two step, schottische, quadrille, three step, minuet, barn dance...I may have forgotten some."

Though my heart was racing from the excitement of anything familiar, I mustered all the calm I could and responded, "I am well acquainted with all but the barn dance." She gently snatched my program and returned, what seemed like only moments later, with every line (except the barn dance) signed for the evening. That worked out very nicely because whoever was your partner for the barn dance was also your dinner partner. I was not anxious to dine with a perfect stranger just yet.

Even though most of the military folk from Fort Egbert had departed the area shortly after the gold rush moved to Nome, there remained a remnant of musically skilled soldiers and their equally skilled wives. As I recall, the band consisted of a bugle, two or three violins, a cello, a piano, and some drums. Later in the evening, for the barn dance, the violins became fiddles and a guitar was added. However, they began the evening with the beautiful, and familiar, "Blue Danube Waltz."

I felt like the *belle of the ball* when the music began. All of my sessions of classes and preparation for my "coming out" came back to me as I glided across the dance floor. I could sense that dancers were stopping and moving aside just to watch as my partner and I moved around the room. A few even applauded that first dance. Later, of course, I learned there are people who always applaud after any dance. At the moment, I gloried in what I thought was a compliment on my abilities, or agilities!

Then the second dance of the evening, the schottische, began. Someone named Frank had signed my program and walked over to where I was seated after the waltz. He held out his hand, which I gladly took, and followed him to the center of the room. The band began 4...1...2...3; 4...1...2...3. My partner ran across the room, guiding me backwards, taking a leap in the air on the second count of 2. At the instant of his leap, I bumped into another couple and turned to apologize, but Frank was already pulling me across the floor after him. By now my hat was being held on my head by only one hat pin. I hadn't a chance to even think about my appearance. I just wanted to stay upright through the ordeal. And that is about all the positive comment one could make about my condition—I was upright! At the end of the dance, Frank guided me to a seat across the room from where I had been sitting by Mother.

All evening, I had been noticing the gentleman I was now sitting beside. He stayed seated in the same spot the entire time. I never saw him speak to anyone else nor even move from his station. I would guess he was a little younger than my parents. Finely dressed in a dark suit and smiling as though satisfied about something, he constantly twiddled his thumbs. I turned to introduce myself to him, but between his occupied hands and my partner approaching for the next dance, I was distracted. Thinking back, I realize that very night I hung the moniker "Twiddles" on him.

Mrs. Myers, recognizing my hat dilemma, rushed over to reanchor it with a couple of pins that remained in the hat. During dance number eleven, the barn dance, I was able to sit by Mother who helped me remove the hat and even held it for me the rest of the evening. Fortunately, Frank did not reappear on my program that night, and I was able to enjoy the feeling of being sociable once again.

It was about two o'clock in the morning before the gentlemen began singing "Good Night, Ladies." Father and Mother had danced the final waltz together and were bundled in furs, waiting for me to join them for the walk home. Oh...there were several men who asked to walk me home, but I reminded myself and informed them that I was a married woman. My husband would probably be returning any day.

As we were leaving the hall, someone coming back inside said, "Be sure to take time to enjoy the Northern Lights."

I wish that I had a poet's heart if for no other reason than to be able to describe things that I see of such amazing beauty. Over the years I have read many narratives and poems and admired many paintings, all of which tried to capture the phenomenal Northern Lights. Yet, none have even come close.

On crisp, clear nights in Eagle, when there is little other source of light, some times the skies perform spectacularly. Often, the lights are only a faint, ghostly green. Yet other times their splendid colors are as varied as a rainbow. Sometimes they appear like a sleeping child, silently and without movement. While at other times they are more like a child at play, crying out "Look at me!" When they are most rambunctious is when words and palettes fail to capture their wonderment. That night was the first of many lifetime nights of being awed by the great *aurora borealis*. Sometimes the lights are ghostly faint, barely visible. Sometimes they are brilliantly colored curtains sailing across the sky as though a window had been left open for a mysterious breeze to cause the curtains to quietly stir. At still other times they appear as enormous columns, dancing across the black velvet of the night's sky. And as they dance, they wander and grow and almost touch the earth and sometimes appear to be solid and other times ever so gossamer. I will take to my grave the memory of that magical night.

When we arrived home, I took my candle from its perch and went directly to Father's "office" desk, the secretary. In the dim light, I could see my reflection in the tiny mirror well enough to take the hairpins from my hair. It was surprising how much my tresses had grown in the months since Rosalind had left. I took the sewing scissors, used only hours earlier for making alterations to the dresses, and cut my hair to shoulder length. In the morning, I would check the trunk for my hairbrush.

Lest I forget to mention that hat again…by late May of that same year, I added enough mosquito netting to the brim of the hat to cover my entire head—a perfect solution to the dilemma of my hat's practicality and my constant battle against the pesty mosquito.

Hannah, Mother, Father and baby Marjorie

Photo from Jessie's Trunk

CHAPTER 8

When I read of Shangri La in the novel *Lost Horizon* by James Hilton, I think of Eagle City. The novel is a story of a little-known community hidden in time and space to which there is only one entrance and exit. This is exactly descriptive of Eagle, Alaska. For virtually all the years I lived there, the only means of entry from "Outside" was the Yukon River. In the winter, travel would be by dog sled or sleigh or snowshoe or afoot. When the River was liquid, myriad and sundry floating vessels were used as transportation. By the mid 1930's, our community was accessible by small airplane.

At Eagle's location, the Yukon River flows north-ish. Newcomers, or *cheechakos,* tend to get confused because "down river" is north and "up river," to Dawson City, is south. Another fact that is befuddling to many visitors is that Eagle is part of Alaska, American soil, and Dawson is in the Yukon Territory of Canada. I know that when I was waiting for housing at the Sitka Pioneer Home, I stayed at Saint Ann's Hospital in Dawson not even thinking about its British connection and, yet, I was afraid to travel through Canada to move to Sitka for fear of not being allowed back onto American soil. But, now, I am really getting ahead of my story.

Eagle's population fluctuates between seasons as well as between years. It was known to have swollen to over 1,000 residents in 1898-99, during the gold rush. During World War II, everyone was frightened that Alaska was in close proximity to the enemy and moved away. By the time I moved to Sitka in 1954, the population of Eagle City was rumored to be below twenty. The city center established in 1897 remains the hub of activity for the town, whatever its population.

As far as I know, the roads are still unpaved. I do not recall Eagle roads before the automobile. I do, however, remember the first airplane. Our mayor declared a holiday for its expected arrival; the entire population turned out to witness the arrival of the first aeroplane on the lawn at Fort Egbert. The bush pilot delivered mail from Fairbanks – letters that had been written that very same morning. Then he hopped into his airplane and loudly gained enough speed to lift the wheels off the grass. Everyone stood around watching the departure until the airplane was almost out of sight. Then it made a sharp turn downward and crashed almost at Fortymile. Thus history was made in Eagle. The first airplane and the first airplane crash were the same date. The pilot escaped unscathed.

I have always tended to be a home body, preferring reading and cooking to hunting or fishing. However, invite me on a picnic or other social gathering – be it dancing, singing, cards, church, or whatever – and I am like the lead sled dog, eager to begin the journey.

The social life in Eagle in the early years was greatly influenced by the Redmen Lodge and the Arctic Brotherhood. But that was not the entire scene. Almost any given night, someone was playing Whist or Pinochle or Pedro or other card games. Keeping in mind that the community was cut off from the rest of Alaska with few exceptions, we provided our own society.

One would wonder how we managed to survive in those early years. My standard answer is, "You do what you have to do. You meet each new day as it comes and not before." Mother was too frail and weak to be of much help. I am not saying she would have been able to help even if her health were better. Father himself admitted he was not very practical. I have a wonderful photograph of him standing by his stack of firewood which gave him occupation enough to stay in fine trim. In another picture, he is wearing a parka, heavy mittens, and boots laced up to the knee. He was quite a marksman, which came in handy for gathering meats. However, once he had shot and bagged his prey, he hadn't a clue of how to dress it. I had to learn the cleaning process as well as cooking.

Although only three miles upriver, Eagle Village seemed to be in another world. I have photographs of their regalia-dressed young men dancing and certainly was acquainted with most of that community. My closest acquaintances from the village were Elizabeth and later my dear friend Borghild Hansen. Besides being our cook, Elizabeth taught me about gardening, cooking meats, drying fish, and native skills too numerous to name. Even Father picked up on her method of drying fish and tried to earn a little supplemental money by selling it.

Generous people from the town shared with us caribou, moose, beaver, bear, porcupine meats, and occasionally dall sheep. The first full summer of our residency, and almost every year since, I planted a garden of flowers and vegetables. Over the years, I have tried my hand at many vegetables such as carrot, potato, turnip, parsnip, polk, cucumber, cabbage, chard, beans, peas, lettuce, perhaps others with varying degrees of success.

The church in Eagle City was either Catholic or Episcopal or Presbyterian, depending on what priest or minister was in town at the time. A small number of us would gather for worship. Immediately following worship, we would go to a small attached room where we would have refreshments and argue the finer points of doctrine for many hours. It was great fun!

Shortly after Albert and Hannah's baby Marjorie was born to their family, they moved to Eagle thinking they could assist our family. Hannah was a tremendous help. She taught me about "home" (England) cooking and housekeeping. I found early on that I enjoyed cooking, and others enjoyed eating what I had prepared. Food preservation had been simple thusfar—thanks to a very cold winter and to the fact that I had not yet had to filet or butcher the catch. I kept copious notes and even entered my knowledge of preparing soup in Mother's journal for more permanent keeping. I'm sure that journal is in the trunk.

Hannah's biggest task during their Eagle residency, besides watching after her little ones, was to work with me on adding and subtracting, and keeping track of money. She tried to introduce me to multiplying and dividing but with little success.

It did not take them long to realize Albert's electrical engineering skills were wasted in Eagle since there was no electricity. They missed their house and friends in Dawson City and moved back to Canada after only a few months with us. I remember especially missing the sounds of children.

For a few years, only two school-age children resided in Eagle City. They were sent to Dawson to boarding school. At the same time, Eagle Village had a full classroom; Mrs. Graves was their teacher. Beginning in 1918, I was hired to clean the Eagle Village school. I also worked for Mrs. Scheele, and others, keeping house and doing laundry. That helped a little.

After the hair disaster, I let my tresses grow long again, and I figured out a way to use sticks for curling. Usually when I curled my hair, I would have to sleep with the sticks in place. Not only was that uncomfortable; I was also a frightful sight!

Transportation was simpler in the wintertime after the River froze over. To walk about, one would strap on snowshoes or skis. To travel any distance, there was always the dog sled. Most people who owned sleds seldom rode on them. That would tire the dogs too much and hinder making any distance. Most trappers used the sleds when checking their lines, but sleds were also the choice of transporting our mail from Dawson City. From Eagle, the mail went north to Circle, some 162 miles away and then on to Fort Yukon and Fairbanks. After "break up" of the frozen Yukon River, mail was transported by steamboats via the river.

Breakup is just one of many indications that the country is about to wake from a very long, dark snooze. Before the snow even begins to melt away, the pussy willows sprout their buds of fuzzy hairs. Slowly, but ever so surely, the daylight hours lengthen, bringing hope of new life. And with that hope came my first mail from home. Alice wrote on the back of a postcard with her photograph "Merry Christmas and a blessed New Year. Cousin Alice."

As the sun crept over the horizon, I woke earlier and yet my expected labor was lessened because I could now go to the community wellhouse for "running water." Also, I did not have to be as concerned about heating the house. Of course, everything inside reeked of wood smoke. The morning sunlight that streamed across the river through the facing windows revealed dustings of ashes covering everything! There was much to do, but the light and warmth inspired me to finish my tasks indoors early in the day, leaving me enough daylight to explore the town and to sit on the porch and appreciate the surroundings and to ponder the past year.

Looking back, the first winter was the most difficult. Yet, I was so busy learning and doing and trying and failing and gaining and, sometimes, even succeeding that it seemed almost sinful just to sit and watch the river and its traffic passing by while visiting over a cup of tea.

Like any small town, Eagle had its rumor mill. And no character in all its history fed that mill quite like George Matlock. He was an early resident, coming down river from Dawson City with his mining partner Frank Buteau. Early on, the two of them built a reputation as aggressive gold miners. They were the first to try hydraulic mining in the region. This required heavy water pressure. Mr. Matlock and Mr. Buteau, early on, dug trenches and ditches to increase the flow of water into pipes and nozzles to wash away the gravel into sluice boxes. Apparently, they were somewhat successful at retrieving more than the average of $800 of gold per year from the region.

Mr. Matlock was a man about my father's age yet opposite of Father in personal hygiene. Partly because he chewed tobacco and partly because he was a trapper (but I suspect mostly because he never bathed), his odor preceded him even in the great outdoors. All his life, he was loud; some would even call him verbose.

The most likely first rumor one heard about George was that he left his Iowa home at age seventeen and hunted buffalo on the plains of the Dakotas and Montana or that he killed a man in Montana, and that was what brought him to the North Country. The next rumors usually centered around his marriages. Wherever he lived, he would marry an Indian woman. In Montana, the story goes, he traded a gun to marry an Indian woman, and, when he departed that country, he returned her to her father.

One of his many mining partners was Franklin Gulch. Mr. Gulch would relate how he and Mr. Matlock once went to Nulato, Alaska, and each returned with "a native wife." Mr. Matlock often bragged about Maggie, the native woman he married in Ketchumstock. "She was the best of all my wives," he would brag. "And to prove it, I married her twice." I know for sure he married a white woman when he was mining in Dawson.

Billy Mitchell, who later became famous as an aviation hero, had been dispatched to Fort Egbert in charge of the daunting task of putting in the telegraph line. According to his sister's account in her book *My*

66

Brother Bill (Harcourt 1953), Billy told about meeting up with one of Eagle's citizens in Seattle. While *enroute* to Alaska, Lieutenant Mitchell was dining alone. He was enjoying the atmosphere of low lights and soft music when a clamorous noise drew his attention to the dining room entrance.

The intruder was described as "a huge, shaggy man in tattered, dirty buckskin shirt and pants." He trod directly to Billy Mitchell's table and seated himself, pulling out a tapestry-covered chair to use as a footstool.

"The name is George Matlock," the big man declared. Billy Mitchell was surprised to learn that he had just come from Eagle, Alaska – the very town to which Billy was being assigned. In the course of conversation, Billy learned this was the first time George Matlock had ever seen an electric light, a streetcar, or an indoor water closet.

Without hesitation, George Matlock placed his order by bellowing, "I'm hungry. I want something to eat. Bring me $2,000 worth of ham and eggs." At that instant, he pulled a bag of gold from his clothing and threw it on the table.

Lieutenant Mitchell's story continues the next morning and for several days following. He told how George Matlock, finely (though not tastefully) outfitted in a new suit led the entire imbibing population of Seattle from one saloon to another, buying drinks for any takers. When every buckboard, street car, automobile, horse, buggy, etc. was filled to overflowing, some twenty or so hearses were added to the traffic with George Matlock at the lead, financing the entire celebration.

Others wrote about George Matlock, also; and myriads of others bore the rumors. No matter what one said about him, in the end, they always managed to show him respect for his uncanny ability to find the gold.

Other local characters mentioned in the rumor mill were the co-owners of one of the local mercantiles, Charles Ott and John Scheele. Mr. Scheele was a quiet, unassuming tinsmith by trade before his wife convinced him to buy into the general mercantile trade in 1908. He purchased John Paulson's share of the Paulson and Ott Trade Company and changed the name to Ott and Scheele. No one who knew Mr. Ott was surprised to see his name appearing before Mr. Scheele's.

Much could be said about both men, but I will mention only of Mr. Scheele that his wife was very much involved in his share of the business and many other aspects of life in Eagle. Most of our dealings were with Mrs. Scheele and with Mr. Ott.

If truth be told, Mr. Ott was often the grinder of the rumor mill. The first encounter I had with Mr. Charles Ott was typical of meetings to follow. I had walked by his residence/business many times without realizing what goods lay beyond those walls, but I had been told that if there was anything I needed or wanted, Ott & Scheele was the merchant to approach.

This particular day, I had just been paid for cleaning house for Mrs. Myers and had coins jingling in my pockets when I came upon Ott & Scheele's business establishment. Out of curiosity, I turned and walked up the path to open the door, but just as I put my hand out to open the door, a gentleman, laden with string-tied brown paper packages, burst out the door and down the path almost knocking me over. As I entered the storeroom and approached the counter, I was pressing my skirt as though that would remove wrinkles and dust and bolster my confidence. When I looked up, staring directly into my eyes was a pudgy fellow, wearing a white shirt with a bow tie and a muslin apron dusted with flour and various sundry other products he had been handling. "Well, and how may I help you this fine day, Mrs. Barber?"

"Have you any books or magazines or newspapers from England?"

"Indeed, we have! What would your preference be? The *London Times* came in the shipment on yesterday's boat. I know you must be pleased to hear that the war is ending. I assume this means you will be returning home in the near future. But, then, I hear too that your father has purchased Mr. Smith's house. And he even spoke with Mr. Scheele about mining with his partner on our claim. This does not sound like a man who is about to leave town."

"I believe I will take the *Times*. How much do I owe you?"

He told me the amount of my purchase, then added, "I heard that you are trying to locate Mr. Barber. Will you be joining him or perhaps returning to your maiden name?"

I avoided eye contact as I counted out the required coins and took possession of my purchase. Upon departure, I was thinking to myself, *It is one thing to talk and learn about others but an entirely different feeling when one realizes she is part of the gossip.*

One thing I learned about Mr. Charles Ott early on was that he had a fearless nature when it came to confronting anyone....especially if the individual owed him money.

Rev. Fred Drain leaving Eagle,
March, 29, 1921.

From Jessie's Photo Album

CHAPTER 9

In early summer 1918, Father bartered his pocket watch to gain boat passage for us to visit Albert and family in Dawson City. We were to stay four days.

"So," teased Albert at the dinner table on the last evening of our visit. "When will you and Charley Ott be announcing your engagement?"

"What makes you think there is any romance between us?" I twitted back at him with a wink.

"I don't know. Maybe because everywhere we went in the months Hannah and I were in Eagle, there he was."

"You exaggerate! The same thing could be said for a dozen men in Eagle, if there were a dozen unattached men in Eagle. It's just that we all have much the same social life."

"I beg to differ with you. Just look at your photographs. You will notice old Charley lurking somewhere in the background."

Making a mental note to check on Albert's claim, I enjoyed our sibling banter. But, alas and alack and wail away, Father and Albert had difficulty being civil to one another.

"Well," Father told Albert over dinner, "I was hoping you would care enough about your parents and sister to at least check on us occasionally."

"I have been unable to afford any time to come to Eagle, but that does not mean I do not care. I care deeply. However, my wife and children must come first."

"You are aware, are you not, that we have been without funds from England for some time?"

"Father, you look as hearty as ever, and I notice that Mother still wears her jewelry. Do you need help? Because I can afford to help some."

"There is no need for you to even offer. We have paid for our transportation back to Eagle. We will be fine."

"Well!" Albert said glancing up from his plate of food, looking each of us in the eye but lingering once his eyes met mine, "We have something we need to tell you. Hannah and I have decided to return to California. The weather is less severe, and even though the pay is less, it will cost us much less to live in Kennett."

Silence hung over the room as every one present shuffled the food on our plates, avoiding one another. I finally broke the silence. "When do you plan to move?"

"I am waiting to hear from the foreman of the Mammoth project in Kennett. If there is still work for me, we will leave immediately."

And, with that note, Father excused himself from the table. Nothing more was mentioned except the formal "goodbyes" the next morning.

When we arrived back in Eagle, a telegram from home brought the wonderful news that Father could now apply to reclaim his fortune from England. Meanwhile, he and Mother went to the notary public and changed their wills. Ulysses Grant Myers signed as a witness of the documentation. They each willed to Albert "the sum of twenty-five dollars." The remainder of their estates and properties was to come to me.

The year of our Lord 1918 was a banner year for folks in Eagle City as well as the rest of the world. The world knew and cared that the Great War was ending. On the other hand, they neither knew of nor cared that Eagle's population was changing. New people were moving their worldly goods to our little community; some we were glad to gain; others, not so glad. Our social life consisted of greeting and feeding visitors in our home, the Redmen Lodge and Arctic Brotherhood gatherings, church, spending time in one of the roadhouses, reading, learning new card games and "calling on others" or, in American terms, visiting in others' homes.

In late August, I was involved in preparing a surprise "going away" celebration for Mrs. Myers. She was going home to Poughkeepsie, New York, to visit family for the winter. I went early to Redmen Hall to set up our gramophone and decorate the hall and to practice playing my violin with the Victrola recording of *Mendelssohn's Concerto in E Minor*. At first, I thought I was alone in the Hall, but the unexpected sound of a man clearing his throat caused me to jump. Turning in the direction of the sound, I could barely make out Twiddles and someone seated beside him. I spoke to them from across the room but went on with my practice.

Later in the evening, I was seated between Twiddles and his guest. I cannot fully describe the excitement I felt when I turned to speak to the stranger. He smelled of fresh soap! I tried to breathe deeply so as to remember the moment, lingering to take in the long lost pleasure of the fragrance of clean. At last, I caught myself day dreaming and quickly began a conversation. How foolish I must have looked!

"My name is Jessie Barber."

"And I am Archibald Herbert Mather, but you may address me as Archie."

"What brings you to Eagle?"

"I have come at my uncle's bidding to learn the trade of trapping. I have been fascinated to learn about my Uncle Ervin from the time I was born. Now I have come to meet the family legend *tete a tete*. Oh, I apologize for slipping into French, please forgive me."

"*Au contraire!*" I replied, and continued the conversation in French. "I am thrilled to meet someone who knows the French language – one who pronounces it correctly. Tell me about your family and from where you have come."

He changed the conversation to English, in consideration of his uncle, "I left my mother and young sister in Vermont, my home state."

"That is why I know your name! Are you related to Cotton Mather? He was the minister and great orator of the Olde North Church."

"Yes, he was my great grandfather." He hesitated then admitted. "Actually, I have no idea of how many 'greats' back he was...perhaps eight or ten."

At this point in the conversation, I was interrupted to play my piece; and I had to excuse myself. I was certain that I would again see Mister Archibald Herbert Mather, Esquire, and his Uncle "Twiddles." I wondered to myself if Twiddles was also a Mather.

That night, I slept fitfully...thinking of the fragrance of a well-kept gentleman and wondering just how old he could be and if I would see him again. In all honesty, I did not notice his facial features or how tall he was or even if he wore shoes. I did, however, remember that his middle name was the same as that of my husband. I thought to myself as I drifted off to sleep, "I must talk to Father about dissolving the legality of a marriage that is not...nor ever was."

The next morning, the steamboat came upriver from Nation, and much of the Eagle community was there to say "Goodbye" to Mrs. Myers and to check for goods or mail that might have come from the North. Mrs.

74

Myers planned to be gone the entire winter. We would miss her company. Within a week after her departure, the first snowflakes dusted the grounds around Eagle. Sitting at our dinner table, Mr. Myers announced, "I've decided to join my wife in Poughkeepsie for the winter. I have no business caring for that enormous house alone, and my mining ventures can wait until springtime." And, so it was, that we loaned him one of our many trunks for his travels, helped him pack, told him we'd watch after his sourdough starter and said our "Fair thee wells!" as he caught the last passage to Whitehorse for the winter. Later, when he reached Skagway, he booked passage on the next ship going south. A trapper heading north with his dog team brought news to Eagle that the *Princess Sophia* had sunk near Juneau. We did not hear that the ship's roster included our Mr. Myers until Mrs. Myers telegrammed that her husband was onboard the ill-fated vessel.

The news, as we heard it, was inconsistent, but, over time, I was able to piece together these facts: On Wednesday October 23, 1918, the *Princess Sophia,* laden with gold, pack horses, and capacity of passengers trying to beat the fast-approaching winter, left Skagway for Vancouver, British Columbia. Within hours of its departure, the vessel ran aground on Vanderbilt Reef. Bad weather and low visibility were blamed for the catastrophe. An SOS was sent immediately, and smaller ships rushed to assist. However, the captain felt his ship was in no danger, being firmly planted on the rock. He wanted to wait until daylight and a diminished storm before transferring passengers to the smaller vessels. Pounding waves finally broke the ship's hull and the ship sank overnight with the loss of all 368 aboard. Mrs. Myers returned to Eagle the following spring to settle their property. Father purchased their dog sled, and Mrs. Myers gave me her cook book. It was all the more difficult to say "Goodbye" this time. It did not take Father long at all to discover the care and keeping of a team of dogs required more time, energy, and food than he cared to exert.

Around this time, word was received from England that my marriage to Bertie could now be annulled for a fee of $150 American. The exchange was arranged by Mr. Ott through the Bank of Montreal. So it was that Mr. Ott was the first to receive the news that I was now Miss Fox again. Father, too, was notified by the accounting firm in Sheffield that his applications for access to his riches had been received.

When the word came that our lives might now return to normal, I began packing crates and trunks (both mentally and physically), dreaming of green fields and brick buildings covered with ivy and walks in the park and leisurely sipping tea and eating cucumber sandwiches and *tete a tetes* with friends back in England. And yet, nothing could have prepared me for the announcement Father dropped on us next.

Just about the time Father was paying off the many debts we had accumulated, he told me that he had news to share with the family after dinner. Then he requested that I fix a special meal and that I not invite any guests. He started for the door, but turned as he reached for the screen, and spoke quietly, almost inaudibly, "Set an extra plate."

I wondered who would be coming to dinner and what Father was up to. I thought about the possibilities. *Could it be Judge Wickersham or the Chief from Eagle Village or perhaps someone from England or, maybe, Twiddles and his pleasant nephew?* I guessed as I readied the house for company and prepared a meal as though the King himself would be sitting at our table.

The menu for the meal was simple—whatever we had. Mrs. Fullerton had given us a moose roast and some flour, and I had the last of my past year's vegetables; I knew I should be planting this year's crop now; but with my energy being spent on packing for our return to England, I had not even worked the soil for a garden.

The potato eyes were sprouting, and the carrots went limp when I picked them up. To revive them, I scrubbed them well and set them in pans of water and chunks of snow from the berm beside the path to the outhouse. To top off the evening meal, I prepared meringue baskets with blueberry sauce that I had canned the previous August.

Then, to add color to the meal, I walked out the front door, past Fort Egbert, almost to the cemetery where I knew the fiddlehead ferns were just at the right stage to be picked. "This guest had better be worth it!" I muttered. When I arrived back at the house, I had just enough time to steam this delicacy. I then went to one of the trunks of foodstuffs we had brought with us and selected a strong lemon tea to serve over the ferns. Early in our residency in Eagle, Father had "used up" any liquors that had been packed. So, I selected a Harrah's Number 10 tea to serve *après* the meal.

As I was anticipating Father and the mystery guest to arrive momentarily, I was pleased with how the table looked. Mother's freshly starched and ironed Irish linen tablecloth with matching linens, my Royal Crown Derby china, polished silver eating utensils and tea service, and crystal wine glasses filled with "running water." Even the food dressed the table nicely: platters of moose and porcupine meat surrounded by potatoes and carrots, my favorite serving bowl filled to the brim with fiddlehead ferns, sourdough bread wrapped in a linen cloth and placed in a Hoopa Indian basket from a long-ago visit with Albert in California, and the *piece de resistance* highbush cranberry sauce for the meat. I rolled the tea cart, laden with dessert and the sparkling tea, next to where I would be seated, nearest the kitchen.

Father came in promptly, muddy but with a huge grin on his face and went directly to his room to clean up. I wondered to myself, *there hasn't been rain for weeks. Where would he have managed to find so much*

77

mud? However, I dared not ask. Father came down to the dining area with his best shirt with freshly starched collar and cuffs and sat at his place at the table. Mother and I joined him and sat quietly for what seemed like an eternity before Father spoke. "I think we should wait a bit longer. Our guest is probably delayed for some reason. He has assured me he would be here this evening." And so we sat…and sat…and sat. Of course, the dinner was cold, and I was so exhausted from its preparation I actually caught myself dozing. By dusk, mother had given up and excused herself to go to bed.

It was actually getting dark outside when the sound of heavy footsteps alerted us to company coming. Father jumped up from his seat and strode quickly to open the door even before the guest could knock.

Before opening the door, Father spoke to me over his shoulder, "Go. Ask your mother to join us." I ran upstairs to wake Mother and straightened her hair a little before leading her down the narrow stairs. When we entered the living room, I realized I had not lit any lanterns. Because the room was dark, I could not tell who the guest was. I could just make out the figure of a man and could tell that he was quite tall. I can honestly say, "Nothing could have ever prepared me for whom Father had invited to dinner." Our invited guest was George Matlock! *Why would Father even speak to him much less befriend this man whose smell and reputation preceded him? This person of such tarnished character?*

"I have wonderful news!" Father began. "I have purchased a mining claim on Fox Creek. Mr. Matlock, here, has agreed to be my partner. My part in this association will, of course, be mostly financial. Whereas, Mr. Matlock will teach me from his experience as a placer miner. He has the reputation of being one of the most capable miners anywhere."

"And our return to England, Father," I asked shakily. "When will that come about?"

"You and your mother may go anytime when the mine pays off. Meanwhile, the two of you can enjoy a life of leisure right here in Eagle."

Etching of the Gardener's Cottage
At Cherry Tree Farm
By Jessie
From Her Trunk

Albert working at Holt and Gregg Quarry, Kennett, California

Photo from Jessie's Trunk

CHAPTER 10

It must have been late January or so when the Federal Census taker knocked at our door. I remember because when I opened the screen door and took a step out to hold it open to admit her, the sun was just coming up. When she left, perhaps an hour later, all was darkness again. This seems strange that it is so fresh in my memory, and yet it was a pivotal moment in my life.

"Do come in. I was just preparing a pot of tea. Would you care to join me?"

"Oh! Thank you so much. I am not supposed to socialize with this task. However, they tell me it is forty degrees below zero. Br-r-r-r. I will accept your offer of tea with the understanding that this is not a social call."

She paused as she fussed with her papers, then continued, "Do you live in this big house alone?"

"No. My parents abide here also. They are presently next door, but I can fetch them if they need to be present."

"If you will please."

Once Father and Mother joined us, the census taker began her questions. I am ashamed to say I do not recall everything she asked other than name, relation, age, occupation, place of birth, and citizenship.

When she asked, "Are you a citizen of the United States?" I had to answer in the negative. I knew so little about citizenship laws, but promised myself that I would learn more on the subject as time allowed.

After she left, I started thinking seriously about the many proposals I had received since coming to Eagle. Many of the suitors (I use this term loosely) were no better off than I when it came to citizenship. It set me to wondering if Albert may have been correct about Charley Ott's attentions.

I took from the trunk my photograph album. It surprised me to see that Albert was correct! Whether the entire town turned out for a visiting poet or three guests came for dinner and cards, Charley Ott was prominent in many of my photographs. To my knowledge Mr. Ott never married. I know for certain that it was not for lack of trying. He was like a sad puppy, following me around. And, I might add, other women also. My aversion to his attentions was difficult to determine. It was not because he was rough or unclean, as was often the case with so many men of my acquaintance. I think it was mostly because he was so attentive – almost smothering.

I promised myself to give the matter some thought, not realizing others might also be considering my future. At first, I thought Father had asked him to watch over me while he was himself preoccupied with preparations for Fox Creek. However, such was not the case. Now, I am getting way ahead of my story.

When Father did grace the house with his presence, it was to catch a nap or add to his list of essentials for the Fox Creek claim. Eventually, I inherited the task of keeping the supply list for them. We did not see Mr. Matlock during this time. We did, however, hear plenty about him.

"George recommends this. George recommends that. George insists on plenty of rope…or hose…or axes…or saws…or lumber."

"What is Mr. Matlock going to do with all of this, Father?" I asked innocently.

"It has something to do with his method of placer mining. Your mother would be very upset if she heard me discussing this subject with you!" And that would end our discussion on the matter.

The house was entirely too quiet without Father's booming voice. When I was not cleaning or baking or polishing silver or ironing or sewing or mending for us or running errands for the miners and when I was not doing much the same for others in order to supplement our needs, I began to unpack the trunks and crates that had mostly gathered dust the past several years.

In early June, as I was walking home from a housekeeping task, I heard someone calling me, "Miss Fox. Oh! Miss Fox." I turned to come face-to-face with Mr. Hillard. He was coming out of the telegraph office. His attire made it obvious he had been working.

"I was, just this moment, coming to chase you down; I have just received this urgent message addressed specifically to your parents. Is there any chance they would both be at home?"

"Yes, as a matter of fact, Father came in this morning in order to rest an injured foot. May I deliver the message for you?"

"If you promise to not open it without your parents present."

"Consider it so promised."

At that, he handed me a sealed envelope, which obviously contained a telegram. The only thing I could decipher was its place of origin—California.

As I closed the house door behind me, I called out. "Mother. Father. We have word from California!" By the time I found my letter opener, they were both seated at the table, waiting for me to read to them long-awaited news of their son and grandchildren, perhaps even announcing a birth of child number three.

I slit open the flimsy, yellowed envelope and slipped out the single, half sheet of paper. As I unfolded the paper, I could see that the message was brief. I did not take the time to pre-read it before the words slipped from my mouth.

SIGNAL CORPS, UNITED STATES ARMY

Washington-Alaska Military Telegraph System

T E L E G R A M

Kennett California

"Albert gone May 31st in tragic work accident. Funeral and burial June 6. Will remain at home here with Walter, Marjory, and baby Mary. Very truly yours, Hannah."

Devastated, Mother and I wept together at the loss of our beloved Albert. We pleaded with Father to take us to California, but he said it was not a convenient time for him to leave the mine. Mother and I waited until Father would accompany us.

It would be late October before Father could tear himself away from mining. When we did arrive in Kennett, I was able to talk with a Mr. James McGinnis, who worked closely with Albert and witnessed his terrible accident. He carefully and kindly told us the details.

"We came down as usual on the cars. We had two cars. Each one has a brake. One has a rope brake and one a solid brake. Mr. Fox was tending to the head car. On the grade, there is a place called Runaway Point. I spoke to Mr. Fox, 'You better slow down before you get to Runaway Point.' He made no remark; he had been going over this road off and on for a year. He seemed to speed up more than usual. He stayed on longer than he ought to. Mr. Holt, our boss, always said that if we should lose control of the cars, to get off, but he hung on longer than he should. I jumped. We must have been going pretty fast. I could not tell. When I got at myself, I looked around for Mr. Fox and he was down at the bottom of the gulch. I think he jumped backwards.

"I went down to where he was. I helped him all I could. My neck was hurt. He said, 'Tell me how badly I am hurt.' I could not tell him as I was pretty badly hurt myself. I straightened him up and put him in position. I said, 'Why didn't you tighten the brake?' He said, 'I did, I pulled on it hard.'

"I held him on my lap. It was in the forenoon, and I had to go for help for it was probable no one would find us as we were not supposed to be down until evening. Something went wrong with the brake.

"I came down to the substation and they phoned. I made him as comfortable as I could."

I asked Mr. McGinnis, "Did you tell him to jump?"

"I did. I said 'Jump!'. And I jumped. I could not see him. All we had to do was step off. He was a good man and a hard worker."

Father did buy a very nice tombstone for Albert's grave. Hannah seemed grateful for that and for our visit, but Father was antsy to get back to his mining. I later learned that Kennett Dam was constructed within a very few years. Water now covers all that was Kennett. Albert's grave was moved to Redding, California. Eventually, Kennett Dam was renamed Shasta.

I admit I thought Father was being selfish, insisting he needed to get back to Fox Creek. At the time, I did not understand the urgency to get back to mining for gold in the dead of winter. Because Eagle's population grew from returning miners in winter, I assumed that all mining operations stopped until the earth thawed. One thing that most people don't realize is that, during the winter, miners can sink their shafts into the permanently frozen ground and not have to reinforce the sides of the shaft with logs nor the top and sides of a drift or tunnel.

At least two men are needed for the winter operation; they have to clear the snow and unfrozen materials from the surface to start the shaft. They begin by building a fire on the frozen ground. Then, after it burns out, they will use shovels and picks to dig out the thawed sand and gravel before they lay another fire and start the process again. In the Seventymile region of Alaska, the layer beneath the ice and snow is a thick, black, frozen muck.

By the time the hole is five feet deep, it is too hard to throw excess dirt or gravel or rocks out with a shovel. A device is then installed using buckets and ropes. It takes one person in the shaft to build the fires and load unwanted debris in the buckets. It takes another person above ground to operate the mechanism.

Therefore it is a long, slow process to go all the way to bedrock. Some have found bedrock as shallow as 12 feet. Others have spent many long, arduous hours abandoning the shaft at 300 feet below the earth's surface. Once bedrock is hit, the miner continues the same procedure horizontally. Many more times than not the miners hit bedrock and do not find any "color." In such case, they begin digging another shaft. It sounds hazardous, and it is. There are life-threatening dangers in each stage, but particularly the deeper the shaft becomes, the more danger there is. The miner could be harmed by falling into the open shaft or by choking on smoke or fumes, or by falling objects causing head injuries, or by cave ins, or by drowning from water breaking through the face of a drift, or by blood poisoning, or by or by asphyxiation when a gas pocket is penetrated. If one survived any or all of these dangers without finding gold, another shaft needed to be dug.

On our passage back to Eagle, Father met a Mr. D. B. Vanderveer from Sedro-Woolley, Washington. Mr. Vanderveer represented some investors from his hometown and was traveling to the Yukon and Alaska territories in search of investment opportunities. This was not his first such journey and certainly not his last.

Not being privy to Father's financial or business dealings, I cannot say how it came about, but Mr. Vanderveer stayed with us the entire journey from Seattle to Eagle. And, once George Matlock met and seemingly approved of the investors, a new partnership was formed that would change my own life forever.

Father on His Claim

Photo from Jessie's Trunk

CHAPTER 11

One day, with Mother watching from her lovely japanned chair, I opened a particularly heavy crate which had been marked "drawing room" and actually let out an audible "Oh, My!! Mother! Look! My books!" Oh, certainly we had unpacked the family Bible and Father's apothecary library, but here were my own beloved, leather-bound Dickens' collection and Ibsen's *A Doll's House* and *Jane Eyre* and *Pride and Prejudice* and *The Works of Shakespeare* and Dickens' *Pickwick Papers* and *Great Expectations* to name only a few. "Where has my mind been? In mothballs, to be sure! Mother, I have been so engrossed in survival that I had almost forgotten my dearest companions! My books! What bliss!"

I spent the next several days removing my old friends, one by one, dusting them off, touching them, smelling them, reading the Tables of Contents, and occasionally allowing myself the luxury of finding and reading a favorite passage. When I pulled out the *Canterbury Tales*, my memory flowed, haltingly at first, but then smoothly "Whan that Aprill with his shoures soote The droghte of March hath perced to the roote, And bathed every veyne in swich licour Of which vertu ngendred is the flour, and so on...."

"Oh, Mother! How I fought Rosalind for making me learn that dreadful verse. It meant absolutely nothing to me at the time, but now it floods my soul with memories of Chanticleer and the Old Wife's Tale; and the Miller. Oh! I shall so enjoy reacquainting myself with my old friends who were on the pilgrimage!"

"I shall find pleasure reading to myself, but would you mind if I read aloud at tea time?"

She silently nodded her approval. That summer was such an exciting time for me. I hurried through my chores at home. Whenever and wherever I could find any employment, I prided myself as being a thorough and punctual and an independent worker. And I did not mind the labour nearly so much, knowing my old and trusted friends, the book characters, were waiting patiently for me at home.

I did not figure an inexperienced woman was needed at Father's claim. However, it very rapidly became evident that our family would starve to death if someone did not plan and prepare the meals. So, I took it upon myself to take food to Father and the workers at least every week or two. Sunday mornings, I would rise early and prepare a large roast of perhaps bear or porcupine or caribou or moose. Once prepared, I placed the warm meat beside the several loaves of bread I had set aside for the mining camp, perhaps add a jelly or sauce, and climb the ladder to set it in the cache. A cache is a miniature log cabin on stilts built mostly to keep bears out. After church, I would take the basket out of the cache and put it with any mail or orders that might have been filled by Mr. Ott during the week.

Usually, I found someone heading toward Fox Creek who could drop off the packages. However, on occasion, I would take it upon myself to deliver the goods. If I could find a ride on the tractor trail to Bryant Creek, that would put me just above Fox Creek, and I could walk the distance to the claim in about one hour.

One fine Sunday in early summer, as I approached Fox Creek, I was certain that I caught a whiff of baking bread. And, upon first glance, the property seemed so much tidier than on previous visits. Next, I heard a definite alto voice singing (rather lustily) "Oh, My Darling Clementine...You are lost and gone forever...dreadful sorrows..." At the sight of me, the owner of the voice stopped rather abruptly. "Who are you?" she inquired.

I was fairly certain that the creature to whom the voice belonged was a woman. However, the person's hair was covered with a bandana and he or she wore clothing which much more resembled what the working men wore – that is, a long-sleeved flannel shirt with the sleeves rolled up to the elbows and somewhat covered by a vest which was not buttoned; the pants were heavy woolen fabric, tucked into the knee-high boots which were snuggly laced. Skinny as a broom handle, every visible part of her seemed to be freckled.

"No," I retorted, "The question is 'Whom, may I ask, are you?' I belong here."

Wiping her hands on her dungarees, she extended her right hand to be shaken. She began introducing herself. "My name is Annie; some folks call me A. Hick. I keep 'em guessin' if that's my real name. You must be Miss Fox. Doc has told me all about his daughter. I could tell that is who you are by your funny way of talkin'."

"Doc says you could be a nurse by trade just because he taught you so much. I had five brothers and three sisters, and I was the oldest so I had to help my mother out. When I was twelve, some men were traveling through where I was born. First off them fellas told me they were goin' to California to strike it rich. I heard them talkin' and asked if I could tag along. Well...wouldn't you know, they made a wrong turn somewhere or other. Or maybe they forgot to turn at all. I'm pretty fuzzy about direction. Anyway, we ended up in North Dakota. I don't know where they went

91

after that. That's where I took up with George and came up to Dawson City and Alaska in search of gold.

"Have you ever been so hungry you'd eat bone butter? I'll teach you to make it. George is the one who taught me to make it, and he hates it worse than anyone you ever knew. When I'm around the fellas, I can hold my own with cussin', but I'll be real careful around such a refined lady as you." As she said "refined lady," she grabbed the extra folds of garment around her thighs and pretended to curtsy.

I wondered to myself, *Who taught you that?* By now, I had given up on waiting for her to take a breath so I could take my leave. The woman never took a breath!

"George is really smart, 'specially when it comes to finding gold. He has a bad temper so we never work together very long. He has already fired me from this job twice. He is paying me $50 a month to take care of the food and the camp and to keep the fellas happy. Pardon my English, but I know lots of useless words, too."

The thought crossed my mind to say, *The news that George Matlock had made such an offer was like saying, Humpty Dumpty will be seated on the King's throne today!* However, what I actually said was, "How do you do? I am Miss Jessie Fox. My father is the proprietor of this mine."

So, as my mind wandered, I truly wondered how George Matlock had any authority to hire anyone…and to set her salary higher than what I could make at all of my paying jobs. I stood to signal my need to take my leave, but that did not seem to register with Annie. I thought she was starved for company but later realized she was just a talker by nature. I had never met such a creature.

Annie continued "Ya know – I just made some blueberry buckle. It's been a long time since I met another woman. Sit a spell…just pick a rock anywhere; I'll bring the buckle. I hope ya like water; it is the one thing for sure we have plenty of around here." At her bidding, I chose a creekside rock large enough for the two of us.

I recognized the brown paper Annie used as a plate for the delicious blueberry treat as having previously been wrapped around an order from Ott and Scheele's. And the water, drawn directly from the stream by which we sat was dipped and served to me in a quart canning jar. And, yet, this occasion sticks in my mind as one of the best treats I have ever experienced. "Why?" one might ask. And, the truth of the matter is that it was the beginning of my first real friendship in Eagle.

Annie prattled on about having been the oldest of ten children. I figured one must have died because that did not match what she said earlier. She came over the Chilkoot Trail at the end of its heyday in 1900, and, when she reached the winter campground at Lake Bennett, she met a companion of George Matlock who told her they were pressing on for Dawson City if she would like to join them. And then she added, "You know. Three times I almost married. Two times it was George who asked me. Watch out for him. He thinks he is quite a lady's man, and he'll stop at nothing if the reward is gold."

I just laughed and started to thank her for the advice but she was already off and running on other things.

About the time I took my last sip of water before taking my leave, I heard Father and George laughing in the distance and decided to slip away undetected. All the way back home, I kept racking my brain, trying to think if I had ever heard my Father called "Doc" or any familiar name. I was fairly certain I had not, and I wondered how I was going to keep that bit of news from Mother.

I need not have worried, for it was Father himself who told Mother. He had injured his foot and had come into town to rest for a few days while his swollen foot healed. Mother and I were having our tea on the front porch when he joined us.

"Well," he said, "tell me, Your Highness, has your daughter told you all about our little friend, Annie? She's quite a talker, that girl. I've never met anyone who could talk so much and say so little. But she is a worker, that one. Even when no one is around to make conversation, she continues to talk. She's also a plucky one; she actually has given me the moniker of 'Doc'. Can you imagine that?"

Mother looked at him…then at me…with such a startled stare that I feared she had suffered a heart attack. But then she burst forth with such a laughter that we both joined her. Before we knew it, we were all in tears, enjoying the frivolity yet gasping for breath.

Upon another visit, Annie was ready for my company. "There you are! I've been watchin' for ya! I wrote out the recipe for bone butter. I never asked George where he larn't this recipe, but the gospel truth is that he taught it to me. He said the recipe came from one of his Indian wives, but I have always suspected that he larn't it in prison."

This is the recipe for bone butter as handed to me by Annie Hicks. "You need bones from a cow or moose or caribou. Break the bones into small pieces. Then boil them in clear water. When cooked, dip the grease off and pour into a jar. It doesn't look like butter or taste like butter, but you never know when it might come in handy."

"There are times I miss home; Oh, nothin' special. Only there's many good qualities about Kentucky that's not in Alaska. You know it's mighty impossible for it to be in Alaska because they don't have the garden facilities here in Alaska we had in Kentucky. People in that country didn't figure on making money.

"We had all sorts of fruits to eat there, Up in the hollow, the pawpaw trees would grow. And, in the Fall, the frost would fall on them. Why, they were good; they were good to eat. I ate them lots of times."

"What's that? Pawpaw?"

"Pawpaws. Well, then we had a tree, a bush; well, it was tall. Called it a Cucumber. And Daddy had me and my brother go up in the mountains and cut them cucumber trees down. Well, you might call them saplings. And we'd bring them down to the barn and put them in the barn and let the horses eat the bark off of them, you know, in order that it would make the horse thrive and get along better. The horse would be healthy; they wouldn't have any disease at all and..."

"Cucumber tree. That's something you don't see in Alaska."

"No. I've never seen one since I left Kentucky. That's been many years ago. They were there and I knew they grew on the tree, but I never knew if they were good for anything. Now the pawpaw looked a good deal like a banana, only he's not as long as a banana but he's shorter. You could eat a pawpaw. And then we went to take a sugar tree and put a spile in 'em."

"A spile?"

"You wouldn't know what it was but I know. It would be like this paper right here in my hand, up like that, all the way down, and you'd take an axe and cut up under the tree like that and stick that spile underneath the place where you cut and put a cup down here and the water would run out of that tree down into the cup and it was good to drink.

"What kind of tree was that?"

"Sugar tree. Some people call them sugar maple, but we called them sugar tree. Then we had all kinds of timber growing there – Hickory, black hickory, white hickory, black oak, white oak, ovacots."

"Ovacots. I never heard of that one before."

"Yeah. And then we had the beets, the beech that grew on the beech. And when the nuts would get ripe, we would eat the nuts – beechnuts – they were good.

"And then late in Fall, we'd have persimmons. And the frost on them, they'd get ripe and the opossums were fat. And you know, we sure did eat opossum in the Fall; don't think we didn't."

My friendship with Annie was good for both of us. I took her a copy of "Ladies' Home Companion" magazine the next time I visited and helped Annie find suitable reading materials and practice becoming a more refined individual. I am even now convinced that one cannot make a silk purse out of a sow's ear.

Having heard from every source who had visited Fox Creek that Annie was thrilled I sent the magazine, I decided to pass along to her copies of "The Jane Austen Journal." She was not quite as fond of those. With time, I learned what her literary likes and dislikes were. Her absolute favorite was "Ladies' Home Companion."

Annie proved to be delightful company. She enjoyed teaching me a little about the mining operation and appreciated learning from me how to knit and embroider. Incidentally, I did hang onto that recipe for bone butter, but never put it to any good use.

CHAPTER 12

After the arrival of Spring in 1920, I found myself going out to Fox Creek more often. Not only did I enjoy watching the process of gathering and releasing great amounts of water in order to wash any gold that might have accumulated where there was no longer any water, but I found enjoyment in just picking up a pie pan and swirling a shovelful of gravel, tossing the lighter, larger rocks, then pebbles, then grains of sand until all that was left clinging to the bottom of the pan was black sand and gold color. Oh, on occasion a small nugget might show up but I knew early on that I would not have the finesse to amass any fortune with my level of skills. Father did not want me using the mining equipment.

"It is not becoming a lady to use heavy equipment," he would remind me.

I remember helping Annie spell some words she wrote to Mr. Ott just prior to her leaving:

§ § §

June 1, 1921

Dear Mr. Ott,

Will you please pay for me $.40 to Miss Fox for a parcel. Also, will you pay any magazines she knows for me. I wonder if W. Glasgow paid me and if not George has paid. I hope so for I want to send out our order for July at latest. Try to send me some stockings will you – size 10. We are getting along fine – I've been fired and rehired again. The first month was $50 of course and now it's $100. Glory be. George is also into his second hundred and I need not tell you that it pleases us to be so much nearer being straightened out. I hope the matrimonial bug gets you this year and that you do your duty by making some girl supremely happy. Don't bother to send key or cup, but if anyone will pack a bottle of lime juice I'd be glad. I don't know why I forgot it – maybe B Steel will – also a couple of packages, envelopes and labels. Will leave this open til something else comes up and any one goes in – A.H.

June 5th ⁻ Will you also send me half a package of Lipton's tea for ourselves as the tea here is vile. And within a while I want to make George a good cup for himself. We are also shy on tea, and I expect Burt will be sending for more. I find they are sending that C.O.D. I feel like sending it back, but perhaps will kindly pay it for me. Tumbell arrived today – the 5th, and I got such lovely mail. I suppose you are very busy now – so are we! Please send three pairs of stockings, size 10 if you have them or can get them. I'll send a bear-skin in by Bob Steel – will you mail it for me to father. His address is Mr. J. F. Miller, 30 Exchange Street, Pontiac, Michigan.

I pay C. Torsall five dollars for sauce. I'll give him a note. Dry weather, but G hasn't wasted much time. Let me have a line if anything has been paid.

Best regards, in haste

A. Hick

If my yarn has come from…

§ § §

On July 4th, everyone came to town for celebration. Annie came by the house; I was outside working in the garden. When I saw that she had been crying, I knew not to ask what had happened. She followed me to our door but refused to come inside. "I'm leaving," she said. "And, this time, no one will find me. Our friendship has meant so much to me, and I hope it has to you, too."

"You know that it has. Do you have a few moments? I have something I want to send with you." She seated herself on the porch, and I dashed inside and upstairs to the trunks. There, I quickly searched for just the correct memento, and selected what I thought appropriate. Then I went to Father's oak secretary and, using a pencil rather than taking time to dip an inkpen, scribbled a quick note, something to the effect of "To a dear friend who has taught me much about gold, I would like for you to remember that silver, too, is precious…as is our friendship. This silver token of our friendship is to remind you. May God bless and keep you as you travel through life…Yours quite truly, Jessie." This was the first of many such gifts from the trunks.

I knew Father and George would be looking for a cook for their camp, but I must admit I was surprised when Father approached me with the idea.

"But, what would Mother do?"

"I have thought that through, and I believe that a bed could be moved out to the mine. I suspect she would rather enjoy the scenery. I will talk to her about the idea. We could pay you $100 a month." I will certainly admit that I was sorely tempted when I heard the dollar figure.

He continued, "You know there are investors considering financing the entire July Creek operation. You do remember Mr. Vanderveer, do you not?"

"Well, yes. But why would you need investors? Are we that close to not having money? Will we ever return to Sheffield?"

"I'm getting too old to think about returning to England, and your Mother would never be able to make the journey. If you wish to go back, I am afraid you will have to go alone unless you should happen to marry. There is nothing and no one in Sheffield for us."

Tears welled up in my eyes and my throat felt as though I was choking. The words had finally been spoken. Words I needed to hear, but it was not easy to accept. And, as far as getting married, I had given it some thought. There were, after all, suitors, but none whom I would consider. If I should choose to marry again, I promised myself *This time I will say "Yes" only to someone I love.* Meanwhile, I told Father "Yes" to his offer of paying employment.

There were some from Redmen Lodge who showed up to help with the move to Fox Creek. Surprisingly, in all of the rubble of being moved to Fox Creek by whoever would volunteer, the only one who was even slightly respectful of our plight was George Matlock. Besides helping mother sort through trunks of clothing, china, and linens, I tried to select what a proper English lady would deem important to survival. It was not so much that Mother had no voice after her initial illness, but rather that she lost her will to converse. In her entire life, she had never been one for idle talk. But after the devastating news of not returning to her homeland, she spoke only to Father and, even then, precious little. It took some doing to move her precious chair and bed.

Moving two English women pack rats proved to be a daunting task for the Fox Creek crew. None of the gentlemen seemed happy to be taking their precious time away from seeking riches. Our trunks had been packed for a return to genteel life in England. It took some forethought to repack for life in the Alaskan wilderness, preparing meals outdoors for working men.

I carefully selected a trunk for storage of items that would not be useful in the near future and wrapped the armadillo shell in linens and placed it, along with my postcard album and the urn of water from the Jordan River in that trunk's empty bottom.

"There." I spoke to the disheveled room as though I had actually accomplished some semblance of order in my life.

"Where?" came the man's voice from the top stair, startling me back to reality.

"Oh! Mr. Matlock! I thought I was alone."

"Where is your Mother's bed? "

"I beg your pardon?"

"I brought Bill all this way from Fox Creek to carry your Mother and her bed. I need to be working. Where is that bed?"

"Oh, of course! It is in the other room."

"The feather mattress will probably be your biggest challenge. We had it made right here from Fort Egbert chickens."

He did not reply but rather groaned when he saw its loftiness. He began immediately to figure out how to transport such bulk. It was about half again wider than my single-person bed here in Sitka and some six or eight inches thick.

"If I soak it, the size will fit, but it would weigh a ton." He thought out loud. "I brought plenty of rope to tie that dang thing on Bill. Right now, I need to go feed Bill while I think about this *%^$#(* problem."

"I'd be happy to prepare a dinner for you and Bill." Truthfully, I could not place a face to the name Bill.

"I'd be glad to say yes if you don't try feeding me any more of that grass." I knew immediately he was referring to the fiddlehead ferns I had prepared for the night he was Father's special guest.

"Of course, it's the least I could do." I excused myself to prepare a meal for Mr. Matlock and his friend. When I called him to eat, George Matlock sat himself at the table.

"Don't you want to let Bill know he is included?"

"Just put some oats in a burlap sack. I'll feed him myself."

"What?!" I could not contain my surprise at his selfish act.

"Bill is a Fort Egbert mule. One of three we bought for Fox Creek."

We both laughed hard at my embarrassing assumption. From that day on, that critter's moniker was "Bill the Mule."

Suffice it to say that canoe, pole boat, mail carrier, foot traffic, and three mules were laden beyond capacity. Shipment for the remaining cargo was arranged through Ott & Scheele.

Bill the Mule was piled high with bedclothes; Mother's feather bed had been stuffed into a barrel lashed to his side. Mother, perched atop it all, was clutching her china tea pot and looking every bit the part of "Her Highness" – not a hair out of place.

At the time of our move to Fox Creek, I did not realize how fortunate we were to enter the camp in late summer. The snow was entirely gone, and many of the boulders had been sorted. After the rocks are moved, the gravel is run through a sluice box to sort out the smaller rocks and sand. Naturally, if there is any gold, by pure weight, it will be buried beneath the final layer of sand or silt. One drawback to the timing was the constant presence of mosquitoes and other pests such as no see 'ems or white socks. Even removed by time and distance, I find myself completely bereft of words to describe how man and beast can go completely mad trying to escape being chewed alive. In recent years, I've been told the mosquito is Alaska's State Bird, and I do believe it.

Often referred to as "poor man's gold," I do not know how placer (pronounced plasser) mining got its name, but I would surmise it had something to do with the placement of gold so deep that no human would even attempt to extract it from the earth. The trick to knowing where to search for the elusive ore is not in knowing where the streambeds are at the present time but rather where they were eons earlier.

The prospector might spend months studying, thawing, digging, picking, sorting and extracting from the earth boulders, then rocks, then pebbles, then sand to reduce the size of rubble for panning. The last tailings from the ends of the sluice box are removed for panning. Father enjoyed the panning process and chose to spend much of his mining time in the more rewarding final stage.

The sluice box consists of a long box, open at the lower end with riffles placed across the width. The upper end is placed high enough that the water flowing down the box will carry the rocks and dirt down to the lower end and out. Sluice boxes are generally quite long because they work by gravity, causing the water to flow down them. The gold settles to the bottom, being two to three times heavier than ordinary rock. The riffles would then be removed and the remaining material, along with the heavy black sand is panned to collect the gold.

George Matlock had advised Father that Fox Creek region had done fairly well in the past. I think that Father felt that because the Creek bore his name, it was a good sign of riches and fame to come "Father, would you teach me about mining?" I pled my case more than once.

"No lady in my family will ever do such physical work!" His reply came quickly and forcefully.

At Fox Creek, I set up housekeeping in a dilapidated cabin. Father and Mr. Matlock were not there much of the time. They were scouting for another claim, or so I thought.

Mother brought with her books and embroidery to occupy her time. Mostly, I stayed busy cooking or keeping order to the camp or reading to Mother.

Mother at Fox Creek Cabin

Photo provided by Eagle Historical Society

CHAPTER 13

For a man almost equal to Father's age, and much larger than Father, George Matlock was strong and seemed to never tire of his quest. He would work long, hard hours, taking only an occasional break to eat. I recall that he once teased me about my British pronunciation of a word, but other than that, there was little conversation between us.

Therefore, when Father approached me with the subject of marriage to Mr. Matlock, it did not seem possible that he was actually suggesting I marry George Matlock. Obviously, Father had given the idea a great deal of thought and was prepared with numerous arguments.

"If I were to die, you would be his partner anyway being that you are basically my only heir."

"Also consider that marrying George would give you American citizenship." It was true that though there were any number of men wanting to marry me, most of them had questionable citizenship.

"He is only slightly older than I am," Father continued. "Considering how he has conducted himself all these years, I'm sure he will not live to be a really old man."

At first, I admit, I was repulsed at the thought of sharing my life, and especially my bed, with George Matlock. However, still yet, obedience to Father was always uppermost in my mind.

One day, when Father was again advising that I should marry Mr. Matlock, I answered, "Why do you think he would have me?"

After little hesitation, Father replied, "For a price, he'd be much obliged."

"And what would that price be?"

"He believes that he would eventually inherit the entire partnership."

"But what about love? I so want to love my life's partner."

"You could grow very old waiting for someone to love. And, too, you could be deported if you do not obtain a citizenship."

Of all the arguments Father had given me for such a union, the one reason that caught my attention and held it was the possibility of gaining American citizenship. If I could just overcome thinking about the rumors about Mr. Matlock's fierce reputation and not allow myself to fear, it might not be so terrible. It was not as though I would truly be a blushing bride; after all, I, like George Matlock, had been previously married. I promised Father I would give Father's proposal some thought.

To marry again was not something I was eager to do, but after some time of mulling over Father's words, I came to see the benefits for myself, especially the coveted citizenship. After all, if I were to not return to England, I would need some security. I pled my case for a wedding dress, and Father said, "Whatever you want. This ditch is about to make us rich beyond belief."

I hurriedly scoured every ladies' magazine available (no matter how old), wanting to find a stylish wedding dress. I finally settled on an all-white silk crepuscule robe and Butterick pattern Number 6050. While he was in the mood, I asked Father to purchase a dress form for me to make fitting my wedding dress easier, explaining that I would be able to use it for Mother and for myself. I named the dress form Gertrude.

I was able to order the wedding dress without anyone in town realizing what was being planned. The day Ed Biederman showed up with Gertrude, the rumor mills started grinding and grew out of control. I'm not privy to much that was being said. However, I do know the words "May and December" were repeated several times. And I know, too, that George Matlock threatened to defend his honor in the matter with more than one gossiper…one of whom may have been an early-on suitor.

November 25 is the date the sun completely disappears for the winter in Eagle City, and the symbolism of utter darkness was not lost on the wedding party. The date for the wedding was set by Father and Mr. Matlock, in deference to their mining. It was to be Thanksgiving Day, but because we still had no snow, United States Commissioner R. E. Steel was delayed in his arrival, which normally that time of year would have been by dog sled.

Robert Steel performed the marriage ceremony in Father's riverfront home on Tuesday, November 29, 1921. There were only six people besides the bride and groom and my parents. A. Froelich and Katherine Meads signed our certificate of marriage as witnesses. When I leaned over to sign the marriage certificate, imagine my surprise to see the typewritten name of my new husband—George *Herbert* Matlock. My second husband and my first husband were both named Herbert.

I had made a traditional English fruit cake, and Father gave us a bottle of fine wine to share. There was neither an exchange of rings nor kisses. Looking at our wedding photographs, one would note there was not even eye contact between us. I had broken my rule of "Next time it will be for love." And I did not expect that to ever change. Our wedding was not a festive occasion. Mother is the only one who even came near a pretense of a smile. I have been quoted as describing the purpose of our marriage as my "going to the mining camp with him to sleep over his potatoes and prevent their freezing." I do not recall ever stating this.

For a wedding gift, Father paid for a journey to Dawson City. We left on Wednesday morning to travel via mule-drawn sleigh up the frozen Yukon River, even though there was no snow and the temperatures had not dipped below 0°F. We checked into the Klondike Hotel and went up to our room. Mr. Matlock had not packed anything for the journey. He went into the room ahead of me, removed his outer coat, took off his suit coat and tie, put his parka back on, and left. It would be two days before he returned without explanation or apology, and without sobriety. He staggered into the room, fell on the bed, and passed out immediately. When he awoke, he said he brought me something. He reached into the inner pocket of his parka and handed me a piece of wadded up newspaper. Inside that paper was a shot glass with the inscription—J E S S I E. That was the only gift he ever gave me. Then he said, "Let's go. I need to get back to work." Thus ended our honeymoon, and, one might say, began our marriage.

CHAPTER 14

Married life to George Matlock was anything but settling for either of us. He had earned a reputation as a capable, though rough, individual. At first, I believed he had married me strictly for the gold, but later I felt he really thought he could become refined. I suppose every marriage requires some adjusting to the other's habits. George detested my dainty sandwiches and the daily practice of tea time. I abhorred his filthy habit of chewing tobacco and spitting wherever and whenever he pleased. He seemed to always be on the verge of an argument or outright fight; I tried, at all cost, to be peaceful.

Father and George had been courting Mr. Vanderveer and his investors from Sedro-Woolley, Washington. It seems Mr. Vanderveer was not happy over their agreement with the owner of the Fourth of July Creek claim. When we returned to Eagle from Dawson, the word was already spreading that the Sedro-Woolley investment company known as the July Creek Placer Company was taking over the operation of the claim. In recent years, the selected region had yielded millions of dollars of gold. Many still felt the July Creek claim was very near the mother lode. Since the main problem was lack of water, eventually George Matlock convinced Mr. Vanderveer to appoint him to be in charge of the operation.

§ § §

11:02 a.m. December 21, 1921

To: George Matlock

c/o Ott & Scheele

Eagle

Will dig the ditch. Make arrangements accordingly. Line up all the men you can. Should have at least fifteen on ditch. Write me fully, if necessary, I can bring in some men with me. Charley Ott, notify upon receipt of this at my expense.

B. D. Vanderveer

§ § §

The Fourth of July Creek is located in the Seventymile region near Nation, Alaska. The ditch Mr. Vanderveer referred to was an itch George Matlock had needed scratching for many years. Some called it an obsession. Because placer mining requires an enormous source of water, which did not exist at the site of the claim, George Matlock had the idea to dig a ditch from Big Washington Creek to July Creek, a rough terrain of some ten miles of brush, rocks, gravel, boulders, and hills.

George Matlock convinced Father and other investors to hire men to dig the ditch that distance, beginning at Big Washington Creek. Mining was all so new to me, but it did not take me long to catch on to the need for water. In January 1922, papers were signed appointing George Matlock as "Alaska Agent" for the quest for gold on July Creek.

I thought Father had sold his property rights to Fox Creek, but later I came to believe that George Matlock had transferred the full title to that claim to himself. This was one of many bones of contention between us. Vacating Fox Creek for good, my granite dishpan was the very last item I placed on the makeshift sled pulled by some of the last surviving mules from Fort Egbert.

Through the rumor mill, we were able to keep up with major happenings in Eagle. The big news, besides the dry weather, was that during the night of December 19th, Eagle's radio station burned down. Nothing was saved. The really big news, according to a letter written to Mr. Vanderveer by Charley Ott himself was, "George Matlock got married after Thanksgiving, and the whole family is down at July Creek."

Father, especially, thrived on the new claim site. On March 25, 1922, he wrote the following in his own hand and attached his shopping list:

§ § §

Dear Mr. Ott,

You will be pleased to know the change here has done both of us good, decidedly it is a quiet place, but beautifully situated in a lovely valley, surrounded by lofty mountains. From our cabin, in every direction we have a clear view of the mountain slopes. So anything moving in the thick small bush wood can be seen.

In this way several times we have seen moose, caribou trails we can see in the snow but so far have not seen the caribou. Ptarmigan have been with us almost all the time by the thousands.

My best pets, the bears, are still asleep but are sure to call on me the first time out. I have a good-sized wood pile here which just gives me occupation enough to keep me in fine trim for meals. Now the winter is past, the sun more powerful, every day, brings me nearer, to what we all know that have lived a few years in this God-made country. It is the most delightful climate in the world, and free from the outside dangers that are killing and maiming someone every hour night or day. Only once since we arrived here have I been more than half a mile from the cabin; and that was two days ago. I went on what my wife said would be a picnic with George, into the woods, to fetch saw logs 5 or 6 miles away on what George said was a perfect boulevard of a trail. I took lunch with me, walked almost all the way there and arrived stiff & somewhat tired. Stumbling along as I had behind the sled in the holes of the mules' feet marks. Well when we got to where the logs are I got my lunch out to have a bite and expected nothing less, but that George would also have some and then soon now we can sit and enjoy a good restful smoke. But no, before I had time to eat two small sandwiches, George was loaded up and started back home again and that was my picnic. Oh, I had a good time, half the night awake with cramps. I am waiting now to go on another picnic.

With best regards to you in which my wife joins

I remain yours faithfully,

Walter C. Fox

§ § §

Nation, Alaska

March 25, 1922

C. Ott, Esq.

Dear Sir,

I am writing this to explain what was left out in my outfit, and also what happened to other portions of it. I could not write before because we had left the bills in Eagle, but when George had got the cases here, and we began to open them, we found that some things were missing. We know these things had been ordered to be sent to Eagle for the invoice to be forwarded and now I have checked it over and find the following things were not sent, viz.

X one gallon honey

X one generator for lamp   these were not sent

X 6 mantles

X one mop handle

X 5 doz. Clothes pins

X one potato masher

3 bottles Worcester sauce   all frozen & burst contents

3 bottles catchup   lost, box not marked

One gallon vinegar   perishable goods

Two clothes lines sent old stock & return broke several times. In place of this send 50 yards of good cord.

Also 5 dozen clothes pins

Send the above down by the first boat, well packed, and make the order 10 dozen clothes pins instead of 5 dozen

        & oblige

        Yours faithfully,

        W. C. Fox

Mr. Ott's response was a bit more terse.

§ § §

March 31, 1922

Mr. W. C. Fox

My dear Doctor:

    I am in receipt of your letter and noticed the shortages you claim. I do not understand it, for I looked all the records over at the day your order was put up, and everything which you claim short was put up and checked. It might be that one box which contained those items was not taken off the boat, but I want to say this that we will make this shortage good, but you have to wait till we have it on hand after the freight arrives here in the spring, for at the present time we have none of the items on hand. Now as to the goods which busted, you can not blame us for that. I was under the impression that you were going down in the fall, in fact Mrs. Matlock was not sure what was going to be done, and it was up to you to notify Mr. Matlock to be careful and look after the bottle goods, as you know when

113

your goods was put up all was in a rush, and we done the best under the circumstances.

 With best regards to all.

 Sincerely,

 Ott & Scheele

§ § §

Father thought it humorous that Charley Ott had referred to us newlyweds in his letter of response to father's letter. Thus set the tone for our correspondence with *Messieurs* Ott and Scheele, suppliers for the duration of the July Creek Placer Company. Though there were other mercantiles we could have done business with, we were already established in our trade and credit with Ott and Scheele. We, and they, knew we were dependent on them.

Particularly, George should have learned a lesson from earlier experiences. In 1889, the *Arctic*, carrying their entire winter's supply of food and equipment, was prevented from navigating the river by early ice. All but George Matlock, Frank Buteau, and two others abandoned mining for the severe winter months. It was rumored that those four men killed forty caribou and survived the winter on meat, some bags of moldy flour, and a few dry beans. Besides being camp cook, I was appointed to keep track of orders.

§ § §

April 10, 1922

Nation, Alaska

Dear Mr. Ott

Will you please send per return by postman Biederman one suit of Stanfield underwear (medium) shirt size 40 in. drawers size 38. (thirty eight) inches also 1 pr. Rubber packs. No. 10 & 5 lb. Master Workman Smoking tobacco.

Will you charge the above to the Company? They are for the men that are working here. Send the bill to me so that I can keep the books straight.

That's all for this time.

Best regards from all

Yrs very truly,

George Matlock (Jessie's handwriting)

§ § §

The rumor reached our camp that Charley Ott was gossiping about our marriage and every little item we ordered. If Eagle would have had a newspaper, we would certainly have been the headlines. Mr. Ott must have been seething mad at us, dreaming up new and hurtful actions to teach us a lesson. The lowest blow came when Charley Ott took it upon himself to write Albert's widow. It had been two years since my brother's tragic accident.

§ § §

May 8, 1922

Mrs. Albert Fox

Redding, Calif.

Dear Madam,

It is really quite a time since we have heard from you, and we know that you have lost your husband, for which we sent you our sympathy. Mrs. Fox, you must still remember that a balance on your account is still due us, we are willing to accept any amount that you can send us every month. But we feel that this ought to be paid to us, as at the time we helped you to live. We know that you received Insurance when your husband died, so at that time our old account should have also been taken into consideration.

We would be pleased to hear from you,

115

With best regards

We are yours truly,

Ott & Scheele

§ § §

May 8, 1922

Nation, Alaska

Dear Mr. Ott,

Will you send down all that you have in the warehouse & the nails by the first boat, the latter, meaning the nails, I did not mention to Van. The balance of the stuff we cannot haul til Van comes anyway & so he can order as he pleases when he comes in himself.

With regards to all from all of us

Yours very truly

George Matlock (penned by Jessie)

§ § §

May 13, 1922

Mr. W. Hunt

Dear Sir:

We have black buttons, but what size do you want, make a drawing of it, or give size. Now as to getting a job over here, there is the July Creek Placer Co. down at Nation, which is 50 miles down river from here; they are going to put in a 6 or 7 mile ditch this summer, and they required some men, how many now I do not know, but if you feel like it, write to George Matlock who is in charge, or you could also write to B. D. Vanderveer. He will be in on one of the first boats; he is the president of the company. Address to either one, at Nation, Alaska.

Very truly yours

Ott & Scheele

§ § §

June 4th, 1922

Nation

Dear Mr. Ott

Your letter received today. Mr. Taylor says everything came. Mr. Van will see to the hauling. Thank you for your trouble. It is quite right to charge anything to George for then it only makes one account & we can settle with him in the fall.

Will you please send 2 cans of talcum powder (good) & two bottles of Freezone & 3 pairs or one of black shoe laces for mother & 2 bottles of glycerin. Charge these to George, too. Mother hasn't been very well. Everyone sends regards. We are frightfully busy. Thanking you for the trouble you have taken.

Yours in sincerity,

Jessie Matlock

§ § §

"This is the worst year I've ever seen for the mosquitoes," everyone was commenting. Some thought it was because of the winter with little snow; some thought it was the location of the mine; some thought it was the lack of water. Whatever the cause, we were all miserable together. It was not so much that the insects would bite, though they certainly did with great regularity. Rather, it was that they would choose to swarm directly in front of one's eyes. There was no relief for man nor beast. When I knew I would be outdoors for any amount of time, I would be completely covered from head to toe—donning hat with netting and gloves and (no matter how warm) one of father's shirts over my dresses. Even that attire did not repel the nagging pests. On occasion, I would see workers run to a rain barrel, the contents of which were supposedly reserved for cooking or doled out for hand washing, and plunge their heads as far down as they could reach without falling in. When they would emerge from this ritual, I

117

could never tell that the insects were any fewer. However, it must have given them at least a temporary relief. I did draw the line, however, if they tried to dowse their dog or work horse in my water supply.

Meanwhile, George Matlock had hired some dozen or so men (mostly miners) to dig his dream ditch. A promised pay of $10 a day was better wages than many of them had ever seen. "How long will it take them to dig it?" I questioned him one day.

It would have been easier to digest if his reply had been simply "None of your beeswax." But instead, he felt the need to curse at me and inform me that keeping books was man's work. I believe he knew better because he had me write most of his correspondence. The main reason he turned the letter writing over to me was because his handwriting and spelling and grammar were all lacking polish (to put it mildly). Also, I believe, the reader would not think the writer was so gruff; though I am certain no one was fooled as to the true identity of the author.

§ § §

August 6th, 1922

Messrs. Ott & Scheele

Dear Sirs

Father received your letter & I would say that I cannot pay the $590.75 until this fall, when I will be paid by the company. Father's letter from the bank was just business, no money came. We have been very interested in hearing about the aeroplane, but you forgot to put in the photo. It was quite nice to think of doing so. An aeroplane would be a boon to travel by the way the trails are this summer. Everyone is very busy & I am glad to say well. Hoping you will understand that I will pay the bill this Fall.

I am

Yours very truly

Jessie Matlock

§ § §

September 29th 1922

Messrs. Ott & Scheele

Dear Mr. Ott

Mr. Van is going to the Landing today & I have asked him to pay my bill for me. I have $400.00 to pay on Father's bill & $100.00. Will you cash for me & out of that would be kind enough to pay Mr. Dover his account. I think it is $42.00 & something. The rest will you send to me in money as I owe Mrs. Meader $30.00 & a medical bill. In a great hurry.

Best wishes from all

Jessie Matlock

§ § §

October 2, 1922

Mrs. Geo. Matlock

Nation, Alaska

Dear Mrs. Matlock:

We duly received the 2 checks from Mr. Vanderveer, and are herewith including the receipted bill in full of Dr. Fox, and your bill showing the amount placed to your credit. Kindly accept thanks for both.

Mr. Vanderveer spoke about the onions, but at the time the shipment left here, we did not have our winter stock in, but we are sending now 50 pounds.

§ § §

October 5, 1922

Mrs. Geo. Matlock

Nation, Alaska

Dear Mrs. Matlock:

Mr. Vanderveer turned in to us the two checks one of $100.00 the other of $400.00. The latter you requested me to credit to you father's account, which we accept with thanks. Mrs. Matlock I want to speak to you in these few lines. I looked the original invoice over and have noticed the set notations made on the side, this was rotten, and that was spoiled, etc. I think it is very unjust to make any such remarks, I have made good this summer all of the shortages claimed, paid also the freight on same. If you remember when you came down in the store, to order the outfit, suppose I had refused you point blank what then. You at that time was not sure whether you would go down before the freeze up or after, and I was not instructed to mark those boxes as perishable. We had to rush to get that order assembled, and I want to say this that at that time we did not put any rotten goods into your outfit. Could I help it if the goods froze, could I keep the onions from rotting? I was under the impression that George would take care of it, as he was down there at the time, and as to all the shortages claimed and made good, they were put up, and sent, but if they were not delivered or stolen could I be blamed for it? I have always done the best with you folks, so long as I could, I don't like the way your Father is acting or has acted, and it is a good lesson to me, this is a partnership business, like any other partnership is, one or the other has the (illegible).

§ § §

December 9th, 1922

Messrs Ott & Scheele

Mr. Charles Ott

Dear Sir

Your letter & receipt of October 5th received early this month. My Father opened a gasoline case & in it was one can of coal oil, the toilet soap, 3 brushes, one potato masher, 2 small cans honey, 1 small bowl, & 36 candles. Those things we could not find. I am returning the letter you sent with the list of things you sent down this summer, so that they can now be added to my account. The notations were made to mention to you on my return. I never insulted anyone in my life and never behind their back. Do you remember when I brought the list down & asked you if I had ordered too much, you shrugged your shoulders and told me I was doing the cooking.

If you had refused the outfit, Mother's & Father's board would have been taken out of my salary. I appreciated the credit as it is best for them to have their own food & I am paying all we owe, as fast as I can.

I wouldn't presume to tell you how to mark your packing & I know nothing was rotten when it left the store.

I thought it right to tell you the shortages, as so many times goods pass the shipping point. I didn't blame you.

The remainder of the outfit for my Father add to my account & it will be paid next fall.

My Father has been good to me & his ways will compare favorably with any father.

Thanking you for the currency & the kindness you showed to them when my brother was killed & Mother has been ill.

Yours truly,

Jessie E. Matlock

PS I can only find the freight bill, you will have a copy of the extra things to charge & that will be alright.

§ § §

December 14, 1922

Mr. Geo. Matlock:

Your postscript makes me smile; it is amusing the amount of privileges and dictating power some imbecilic persons credit themselves with to possess.

The brain of your informer of a Mock Wedding was evidently very much befogged.

The wedding my wife and I, with a few friends present, celebrated last fall was our 25th wedding anniversary (silver wedding). We will have a few friends come to the house this year and help us to celebrate, and to us it is quite proper to observe the day. Anybody who wishes to call it a Mock Wedding can do so for all I care. We reserve the right to celebrate family or any other event we wish to commemorate regardless of outside comment. I have tried herein to fully express my sentiment.

Scheele

§ § §

Looking back, the ditch took more than three years to dig. It was an enormous task, and I was thankful Father was not the entire financial backing. About the time the ditch project was nearing completion, several occurrences brought about change in my life. First off, Father and Mother invited me to spend the winter with them in Fairbanks. Next, George Matlock decided that since I was family, I should not expect pay for being camp cook which added further to the tension between us. And, last but not least, I ran into the adorable Mr. Mather.

Ice Wagon Delivering Supplies

From Jessie's Photo Album

Archie Mather & Ginger

Photo from Jessie's Trunk

CHAPTER 15

Wanting to pick some seasonal blueberries, I had hurriedly cleaned up after the evening meal. I find it difficult to call it supper as the Americans do. Taking my walking stick, a tin bucket, and the camp dog Ginger, I started to follow a creek which led to a stream which led to a brook. I had never taken this route from July Creek. It was late August because the sun was low in the sky by the time I left. Probably within a mile of camp, I found a good patch of berries. Knowing I had at most an hour of daylight left, I went right to work. Ginger faithfully stayed right with me as the sound of berries hitting metal softened. She strayed only occasionally to the nearby brook for a quick slurping of water then would come right back beside me. When the bucket was about three-fourths full, and I could no longer identify the berries because of darkness setting in, I took off my kerchief, tied it carefully around the top of the bucket to keep the morsels from spilling and started to walk toward the brook. That is when I realized Ginger was pointing in the direction we needed to go and lightly growling.

Grasping her by the scruff of the neck, I tried to keep her calm. "If it is a porcupine, Ginger," I said softly, "stay right here." Then, thinking aloud, "And if it is a bear, don't leave me." By then, Ginger's growl had heightened, and I froze in position. I could hear rustling in the brush

125

nearby. I could not see what it was because of my peripheral vision, or lack thereof. Just as I was about to panic, Ginger started to bark and run toward our intruder. Next, I could hear another animal's heavy breathing intermittent with a bark and then a faint whistle. When I turned to look, in the dim evening light, I could see that a man was approaching.

"Well, hello, Miss Fox; it has been awhile since we have talked."

"You are quite right, Mr. Mather. And where is your uncle?"

"He is out checking for places to set his winter traps. I am mining near here. What brings you way out here?"

"I am working as a cook for the Fourth of July Camp. Tell me. Have you come up with any more ancestral quotes?"

"Ancestral? No. But I have recently read Robert Service and found a quote or two to share next time I met a lovely lady. But, alas, nighttime falleth, and I must bid you farewell or else you will become unemployed. Do come to visit me; I have pitched my tent just beyond the crick in the creek." He pointed upstream.

He was so charming and unassuming; I did not wish to leave his side. However, he was correct. I would be in trouble or maybe even lost if I did not get back to camp. He walked me to the creek bed and stooped as if to pick something up.

"*Pour vous, Mademoiselle Renard.*" He spoke ever so softly as he straightened to look into my eyes. He stretched out his hand and in it was a single wild aster."

"*Merci, Monsieur,*" was all that I could manage in response while thinking to myself, *When was the last time I was called* renard *for Fox? Who, besides Albert, had ever presented me with flowers?*

"Fair thee well," I bade him and started my walk back to July Creek. I knew that I was happy to see him again. Also, I knew that I should have corrected his assumption that I had remained unmarried since last we

126

met. After some time, I realized two things. One that I was humming "Ole King Cole" or some other ditty – and two – that I should be nearing Fourth of July Camp by now. I had not worried because tonight would be a full moon. However, I had failed to note that clouds had moved in to cover any anticipated light. I was thankful to have Ginger as a companion for indeed she did lead me directly to camp.

Before bedding down for the night, I still had to set my sourdough for breakfast and soak the berries. I could make blueberry syrup while the pancake batter set. George Matlock was far from my thoughts that night. He was probably on the ditch somewhere and would not be in our bed.

I kept watching for opportunity to pick berries once more before early frost but that time did not come. As the ditch came closer to the camp, demands on my time multiplied. Long after the aster had wilted and I had pressed it in my copy of Ibsen's *Doll House,* my thoughts were constantly on the charming Mr. Mather.

"*Renard!*" "Fox!" How many times in my life had I been called that? Too many times to count. And, certainly, most times not endearingly. Every time I thought of the moment the young Mr. Mather said those words, I could still feel chills as the *r-r-r*'s rolled off of his tongue. Truthfully, outside of reading the Brontes or Jane Austin, I had never in my life experienced such emotions.

Some few days later, I was surprised by a visit from the other Mr. Mather – the one I had always called "Twiddles." Having just finished setting the bread dough for a final rising and having added a bit more salt to the caribou stew, I was just about to sit down for a few minutes to read. That was when I felt the presence of a tall figure, quietly watching me.

"Oh! Hello!" was all the greeting I could muster, mainly because I could not recall his actual name.

"Good morning, Mrs. Matlock. My nephew asked me to stop by and deliver this batch of cotton grass to you."

I grabbed a canning jar, emptied its accumulated debris, and accepted the bouquet of dried fluff for a table centerpiece.

"Won't you join me for tea?"

"I would appreciate that very much," he answered calmly.

When I returned to the table with the pot of tea and a few dainties to accompany the tea, I saw that he was twiddling his thumbs…still.

"What was his name?" I was not sure I had ever heard it. "You are another Mr. Mather?"

"Yes." I recall that was all the assistance he would give to that conversation….and many to follow. For he was a quiet man, a man of few words. I thought him quite shy. However, in later years, I would change that opinion of him to steadfast.

That day, I learned very little about him except that he had left Vermont in his youth and traveled to Canada. Though he had never been a gold seeker; he had traveled with the "gold rushers" making his own way as a trapper. He had been in Skagway when Soapy Smith and his vigilantes ran the town. The reason he had stayed in the Eagle area so long was because his nephew had sought him out and seemed to bring more stability to his wanderings.

In our conversation, we did not mention the fact that Twiddles knew I was married. I did, however, learn that he had worked as a ditch digger for the July Creek project, off and on. I studied his features and could find little physical resemblance to his nephew. He was a tall, lank man; whereas his nephew Archie was not much taller than I and had the physical bearing of royalty. Twiddles was balding; Archie had a head of thick hair, with just a hint of a natural wave. Even now, my heart seemingly skips a beat just remembering Archie's sweet nature. Oh, how I ached to be in his presence.

One morning, I awoke feeling chilled and groped for an extra quilt. I found all of my extra bedding was packed away in trunks, most of which were stored in Father's big house on the river.

I peeked out of the cabin window and was surprised to see frost. *Could it possibly be winter already?* This would mean that the ditch diggers should be working extra hard to finish the last little distance, trying to reach July Creek before the ground was either too hard to dig or completely covered with snow. Several of the diggers had already turned in their pick ax and shovel and headed south.

"Certainly, we will be back by Spring thaw," the miners said as they counted their wages and waved "goodbye."

I realized the days were slipping by. An early frost meant I was already behind in my canning for the winter months. This meant stripping the garden of anything salvageable and drying some things but putting up in jars the majority. While planning and instituting preparations for winter, I kept noticing the fall colors surrounding me and frantically wanted to get to the highbush cranberries before they turned to mush.

Finally, one sunny Autumn morning, I had cleaned up after the few ditch diggers who came for breakfast. As they were heading to the ditch, I sent a lunch out to George. This seemed the perfect day to return to where I had earlier noticed a good crop of highbush cranberries. It has accurately been said that they smelled more like "behind the bush." I well knew that other berries could be substituted in my sauce recipe. It was still one of my favorite pursuits. Their red and yellow leaves would be easy to spot, and I so wanted to "put up" my sauces for meats. I knew exactly where there was an abundance for I had spotted them while picking blueberries some weeks earlier.

So it was that on this glorious, crisp, fall day, I followed the dry creek bed once again, telling myself (and others) I was in search of the foul-smelling highbush cranberry. Yet I hoped to run into the man who occupied all my thoughts. I took Ginger along.

Within shouting distance of the lush blueberry patch I had picked earlier, the tell-tale, brightly-colored leaves beckoned me to gather their attached crop. The highbush cranberry shrub can be another two to three feet above my reach, but they were plentiful. It must have been about 2:00 in the afternoon when I began picking. I had been optimistic about what I could harvest and took a large lard bucket to capture the bounty.

My voice rang out "*La Bohème*" and "*Greensleeves*" as I picked berries. Apparently, neither I nor Ginger heard anyone approaching, but there "he" was stepping out from behind a stand of tall grasses across the creek.

"Good day, M'lady! You are missing the best of the crop. Would you allow me to help in your pursuit?" he shouted to be heard above the water's sound.

"Why of course." I could feel my cheeks flush as I removed the coffee-size can dangling on a string about my neck and emptied it into the lard bucket. The ping sound of the berries hitting the bottom of the lard bucket reminded me I still had a lot of work to do before the shortened daylight ended.

"I will hold the tops of the bushes for you, and you can pick," he offered upon approach. "Your task will go much faster, and we can actually get acquainted in the process." Being the gentleman he was, he removed his hat and began putting berries in it.

"For quite some time, I have wanted to make your acquaintance. You know I spent a little time in London during my youth? I must admit to being enamored with your accent. Tell me about yourself."

And so it was…after eleven years of feeling deserted… I felt someone actually showed an interest in me as a person and in my life. And, I will say it again. That someone was extremely attractive and charming.

"I even acted in a play while in London." He spoke as he moved among the shrubs. "When I was quite young, I thought I wanted to be an actor. However, it was painfully obvious to everyone…even me…that I did not belong on the stage. You may be surprised to learn that I had absolutely no acting talent." He chortled a little under his breath as he continued to pick fruit and to talk. "But, *Mademoiselle*, enough about me; I want to hear about your fascinating life."

"I suspect you may know much about my life. There are not many secrets in a small town. I grew up in Sheffield, England, in a privileged family. I had one brother. Oh, I do wish you could have met Albert; we were very close." I choked, just trying to mention his name. "Tell me about your Uncle Twiddles."

"Are you speaking of Uncle Ervin?"

"Oh! I am so embarrassed. I dubbed him 'Twiddles' the first time I laid eyes on him because he always twiddles his thumbs."

"He is a very giving person. I have been so blessed by his generosity. He is a very private person; I think it has been difficult for him to have me around. He is a very hard working trapper and so capable of much more. However, he wants nothing to do with mining. He says he has witnessed enough lives ruined in the pursuit of riches. He claims most miners never make more than $1,000 a year. I don't know how accurate that is, but I do know I am not coming anywhere near that amount."

"How do you manage?"

"Mostly Uncle Ervin's trapping keeps us alive. Not only is he able to get a fair price for his pelts, he keeps an ample supply of meat, which we can eat or trade for other food stuffs. Up until recently, I had a paying job for fifty cents an hour plus room and board."

Archie looked pensively into the accumulation of berries and wrinkled his brow.

"This picking is going entirely too quickly. Could I interest you in some tea?"

"Actually, no," I replied. "I brought enough food for four people to survive for several days. I even have an extra cup. That is if you do not mind drinking out of a tin can."

"With you, M'lady, the container is of little importance." As he said this, he placed his right arm across his waistline as to bow. And with his left hand, he pulled from his hip pocket a large handkerchief. He walked over to the creek, selected a large, flat rock and spread the cloth.

I picked up my satchel I had made from table linens. In it I had packed biscuits, moose jerky, dried salmon, cucumber sandwiches, and muffins with berries. It made a fine meal, if I say so myself.

"I'd like to know more about you," he said. "You know; I tried to work on the ditch to Fourth of July Creek when it was first started, but your boss was too demanding. Yessir, George Matlock is a real slave driver. How did you ever end up working for that man?"

"Well, you see I own stock in the Fourth of July claim."

"Really!? I had no idea! Obviously there is much I have yet to learn about you."

We sat and ate at a little too much leisure. Suddenly, I realized that the day was getting away from me. I leapt to my feet, stating I needed to get to work. I would pick only another hour, then I needed to head back.

True to his word, Archie lowered the tops of the shrubs, holding them for me to pluck the berries. I will take to my grave the memory of that day but particularly a special moment in time. Archie was grasping a fistful of upper shrubs, and just as I started to pick, a limb escaped his hold. He quickly reached out to restrain the springing limb but instead lost his grip on the entire bundle. Instinctively, he reached over to protect my head. When the excitement of the moment passed, I was still cradled in his arms.

"Are you all right?" He whispered into my hair.

"Yes. Very," breathlessly I answered. Even then, neither of us moved. When he did release me, we were still close enough to feel the other's breath. Archie calmly pushed back a stray tress from my face and leaned over and placed a tender kiss on my forehead. With eyes closed, I was completely motionless, like a rabbit who knows she has been seen and yet staying perfectly still.

"I must go. I have to put up my meat sauce and prepare supper for the workers."

"*Au revoire!*" he said. "Which literally translated means til we see again." He took my hands and kissed them; then he picked up the harvested berries and, with our fingers intertwined, walked with me until Fourth of July Camp was in sight.

"It would be best if you don't come into camp with me. I promise to come again soon."

"Parting is such sweet sorrow, M'love," he declared as he kissed my hand and turned loose.

HIGHBUSH CRANBERRY CATSUP

8 cups Highbush Cranberry
1 pound onion (chopped fine)
2 cups water
2 cups vinegar
4 cups sugar
1 Tablespoon ground cloves
1 Tablespoon cinnamon
1 Tablespoon allspice
1 Tablespoon celery salt
1 Tablespoon salt
1 Tablespoon pepper

Cook the cranberries and onion in the 2 cups water until soft; then put through a food mill or sieve. Add the vinegar, sugar, spices, celery salt, salt and pepper and boil until the mixture thickens and re ches the proper consistency. Pour into sterilized jars and seal. Makes about 3 pints.

Serve with poultry, meat, or on baked beans. Particularly tasty on moose!

CHAPTER 16

My happiness was evident to everyone. I sang more, quoted poetry, daydreamed about Archie's tender touch, waltzed around camp with a broom or mop or stick. He was in my every thought. He was a caring soul and, as it turns out, a gift giver. He loved to surprise me with thoughtful gifts. It was several days later before George returned from a meeting with Mr. Vanderveer.

"I'm tired," he admitted, as he plopped down in Father's favorite chair. "Sedro-Woolley is trying to pressure us into finishing the ditch before winter. And most of the men have already left. I don't see how it can be done before next Spring." This is probably the only time George Matlock ever confided in me. Even then, his language was peppered with colorful expressions.

"What more can I do to help?" I offered. "I feel completely helpless when it comes to digging the ditch;" I said aloud while thinking to myself, *After all, I am holding up my end of this partnership by keeping the food prepared and much of the correspondence.*

George sat quietly staring at what he had often called "my kingdom." He did not lift so much as a morsel of food or drink to his lips. I placed a quilt over his shoulders and returned to my duties. From the very inception of the project, it was difficult to keep workers on the ditch, especially those Mr. Vanderveer had imported from Outside. The hired men could not help but think they could be harvesting gold for their own pockets. This led to problems of being shorthanded and to problems of theft.

Later that same day, when I went to the creek bed to do the laundry, there was a quart jar which held a bouquet of tundra roses, some of which had already become rose hips. There were enough rose hips to dry for tea or seasonings. I looked all around for a sign of who had placed them, but did not see anyone. In spite of other woes, I smiled just thinking about Archie.

When I returned to the cookhouse, George was gone. I was certain he was somewhere along the ditch. I fed his untouched food to Ginger and went about preparing soup for the few men who might show up to eat. Normally, I would have been preparing for winter and the move back to Eagle, but obviously this new development might keep a skeleton crew on as long as they were willing to work.

George Matlock and I could give the appearance of being civil to one another. But when there were rare moments of inactivity, we could hardly abide being together. True to his reputation, he was a task master, expecting the same exertion from others as he did himself. He seldom commented about the food I prepared. He would occasionally tease me about the linens or wildflowers with which I graced the tables.

The weather very quickly turned into winter. We watched the scenic vista as it slowly, progressively turn to white from the hillsides down. We called that progression of snow "termination dust" as we prepared for a long, hard winter. No one could remember ever seeing the changing fall-to-winter transformation this early, but everyone was talking about it. Especially George Matlock. He was not one to admit defeat, but the weather was forcing shutting down digging the ditch until Spring.

Meanwhile, Father and Mother were making frequent visits to Fairbanks for medical help. Finally, they decided to move to Fairbanks to be near doctors. Though they had invited me to join them, I chose to return to Eagle to try to put the riverfront house in order. In addition to normal housekeeping, this would entail checking for what wood was needed, moving logged and split wood from the woodshed to under the eaves by the kitchen; and, if George Matlock were not so inclined, engaging someone to replenish what wood had been used.

The enormous task of making the house livable would begin with making order after Mother and Father's hurried departure to Fairbanks. Following that, I needed to inventory and replace food, clothing, and lighting. Because of the deplorable condition of the windows from weather and aging, it was not as though one could actually see out nor, for that matter, that light could penetrate. However, it just felt cleaner and brighter, knowing the smoke residue and grime were gone.

I had a mountain of clothes and linens that needed either mending or converting to usable rags. And, of course, I must plan for Spring planting and the return to July Creek which would come all too soon.

Because it had been almost a year since I had been in Eagle for any time, of highest importance was the need to catch up on local news and happenings, and I knew just where to go.

Charley Ott was standing outside the front door of Ott & Scheele surrounded by boxes and crates, puffing away on his "Sherlock Holmes" pipe.

"Good morning, Mr. Ott." I interrupted his thoughts.

"G'day," he answered rather curtly, without looking up.

"I have come to purchase a few groceries, but mostly I wanted to catch up on any news you might have. What happened to whom, and who happened to what in our absence?"

"Mrs. Matlock, you are a paying customer, and I do not wish to do anything to dissuade your loyalty. However, I do no longer consider you to be a part of my circle of friends. To put it bluntly, if you were so desperate for a bed partner, I could most certainly have obliged. And you would have had to be extremely naïve to have not known my intentions. So, what merchandise can I help you with?"

"Nothing!" was my simple answer before I turned and stomped off. His words had stung me deeply. I can honestly say I felt betrayed.

Even life in Eagle had not stayed stagnant in our absence. Had there been a newspaper, the headlines would have read "Northern Commercial Buys Ott and Scheele." Ott and Scheele had been the last mercantile on the Yukon, and perhaps in the entire world, to give up their clientele to the powerful conglomerate.

I would say it was probably mid-October; I remember the days were quite short when George arrived to announce he must head South immediately in order to meet up with Mr. Vanderveer; I suppose they met in Whitehorse.

"How long will you be gone?"

"I will be back before Spring in order to work on setup at Fourth of July Creek."

"What about wood for the house and keeping the stove pipe clear. I don't think I can handle that alone."

"Then hire someone; there's plenty of men in Eagle scrounging for work for the winter."

"And how will I pay him? Or, for that matter, how will I pay for anything while you are away? Would you like to bathe before you leave? I could have a full tub of water for you by morning."

"No! Woman. I don't need no bath!" As he threw a sock on the table; it hit with a CLANK, and I knew this was my winter budget.

I stayed up much of the night preparing a satchel of food for George's journey. I was never sure when he left, but I assumed he went with the stage line. However, I learned later that he struck out on foot and got to Dawson before the "stage."

The first day he was gone, I did not venture outside. There was plenty to do to put the household in order, and I was most eager to have some lady friends again. I would begin by having Mrs. Scheele and some other ladies to come for tea. Meanwhile, I would go through my own personal trunk and bring out my china. I recalled Albert teasing me about misnaming it my "despair barrel."

"If only Albert were alive today, I would not be in this predicament," I muttered to myself as I took a break for tea and sorted through the mail I'd been setting aside for months. It just felt good to think about myself for a change.

The next morning, I went to deliver the invitations for tea. The weather was an omen of the winter ahead – cold and very windy with a light dusting of snow underfoot and a promise of much more to come. I had dressed in layers to brave the cold and, at the last moment, had thrown a blanket around my shoulders reminding myself to sort through the winter trunk very soon. My head was covered with Father's hunting cap and a blanket wrapped around my face as I tried to walk against the fierce wind. I will admit that my visibility was hampered.

Without warning, I bumped into something or someone. When I stepped back then to my left then forward, there was the same wall. I tried a third, and a fourth, time. Finally, I tried to take the blanket from my head but it became more tangled than ever.

"M'lady," I could barely decipher above the wind's whine, "Let me help you."

"Oh. It is my friend. Sir Galahad! I have been awaiting your rescue." We both laughed as Archie guided me only a few steps away between two houses for protection from the wind. There, he tenderly aided me in removing the blanket and folding it like a cape and placing it over my shoulders. When I was wrapped securely, he removed a handkerchief from his pocket and carefully daubed my damp face. I could feel his warm breath against my cold cheek, and it felt so comforting.

"I must be on my way." I spoke halfheartedly.

"I must also," he answered as he stepped back. "I am going with Uncle Ervin to set traps. Then, I am thinking I may go up to Chicken to find some winter labor."

"Oh! I am in need of a man to keep the wood pile stacked and the snow shoveled off the roof and paths to the waterless closet and the road. Perhaps you and Twiddles would like to work for me."

"Would it be proper for me to come talk with you about work?"

"I see no harm in that. However, if you want the job, it is yours."

"Then I will begin upon return from setting traps. May I call on you then?'

"By all means!"

"Will you be secure for a few days?"

"So long as the snow does not plug the stove pipe, I will manage fine. I am so afraid of a chimney fire."

"Then I shall take my leave and bid you *adieu* so that I might come and rescue you from the fiery dragon!"

"Ah, indeed, you are truly my Sir Galahad!" I do not think he heard when I spoke into the wind as he turned and left. He always left me smiling.

Mrs. Biederman, Mrs. Scheele, and Mrs. Hillard came after the dinner hour that evening. We played a rousing game of Whist. It is very

140

difficult to find American women who play Bridge. I could not tell you who won the game. It just felt so good to be enjoying the company of other ladies. I more than caught up on the local news. The game ended at 3:00 the next morning. I fell into bed, and in spite of being alone in a house being shaken by gusty winds, I slept soundly.

For the next several days, the house continued to rattle from the wind beating against it. Frankly, even with the fire going full time and full blast, it was impossible to get warm. The knock at the door was barely audible. As a matter of fact, I was unsure I had heard anything but decided to check to be certain.

When I opened the door, Archie Mather removed his hat immediately, his eyes looking downward. I invited him inside to sit by the fire.

He peeked at me with a sideways glance, his eyes avoiding contact. I rushed to the kitchen to prepare a spot of tea, chattering away about the weather and the need for a man to help with the numerous tasks.

Finally, he spoke. "Uncle Ervin tells me that you are married to George Matlock. Please tell me he is mistaken."

"I am afraid Twiddles is correct; I guess I assumed everyone knew." To this day, I wonder how the news escaped Archie. I do now know he was never one to pay attention when folks started to gossip. And he rarely stayed to listen to idle talk unless the conversation involved gold.

"I owe you an enormous apology for forgetting my gentlemanly manners. My mother raised me better than that."

"Absolutely," the words came from somewhere deep inside me. "I thought the entire world had heard about the wedding."

"No, Madam." He said shyly. "I hope you do not judge me."

141

"The Bible says to 'Judge not that ye be not judged.' And I would say that lesson applies to me as well. Do sit. Let us have a spot of tea and talk about the work that needs to be done."

"You mean you still want me to work for you?"

"Of course. I am nearly freezing now. They tell me the temperature is already below zero. I must have some help."

As I spoke, he wrote down the things that must be done. He also noted little tasks that needed to be done – things only a handy person would notice. And handy he was. He could fix anything.

One would think there would not be that much to do in the winter since there is little or nothing that can be done in the yard other than keeping paths cleared to the road and the "waterless" closet and the wood pile and the "ice box." Archie Mather arrived by 9:00 each morning and would faithfully labor the time needed to complete his task.

At 4:00 each day, I would serve tea and crumpets or lady finger cookies or dainty sandwiches. If there were no callers, and if he was still working, Archie could be persuaded to take a break from his work to sit with me briefly. Sometimes we discussed literature. Other times, we would have a rousing discussion of religion; Archie was a nominal Catholic.

Archie and I were developing a comfortable friendship. And, frankly, I was so caught up in the house and Archie that I did not notice there were fewer and fewer callers at tea time. Once, Nimrod came just as Archie and I had sat down for tea. Archie had not believed the story of Nimrod's dentures, and asked him to verify what he had heard. This is Nimrod's own story as he told it to Ernie Pyle in 1912 for the book *Home Country*. "In the winter of 1905, the wolves raided their claim of all meat. Nimrod got scurvy and lost all of his teeth. He made a frame of aluminum, punching holes to set teeth in. For the front teeth, he filed down mountain sheep teeth. For the back, he used bear molars; he only needed one for each side. He admitted to eating bear with those teeth, but not their original owner."

Archie and I laughed until we cried hearing Nimrod's adventures. It has correctly been said of Nimrod that "He could make anything but a living." His incredible relief map of the region is made of newspapers, magazines, and iron ore. Before Nimrod left that day, he checked the crystal clock. It still kept perfect time.

In our banter, Archie would sometimes teasingly say, "If you were my wife…" and fill in the blank with "I would buy you fineries and take you back to Sheffield to show you off." or "I would never leave your side…" or "Your hands would never touch the water of labor again."

When Christmas day came and went, there had still been no word from George. I had gone to the Christmas Ball alone and stayed only through the third dance. Archie gave me a gift wrapped in brown paper. It was a jar for my sourdough starter. I gave him a poem I had copied from a lady's magazine and had painted around it a border of flowers.

Sewing Kit

From Jessie's Trunk

Photo by Rosco Pirtle

CHAPTER 17

As 1924 New Year's Eve approached, I decided to make myself a new dress. I had some fabric intended for a table cover. The house was so dark, it was nearly impossible to thread a needle or sew on dark fabric with dark thread. I usually sat two lanterns near my work. However, this time I chose to use candles. Very late the night before the big celebration, I was just finishing the sewing on my treadle machine when I heard a loud crash at the front porch. I rushed to find the origin of the sound. There, on the porch, lay George.

"Woman, get me some hot water—fast. My feet are frozen."

"What happened?"

"Some blankety-blank fool was tunneling for gold at Fortymile and chopped up the creek bed. I stepped in it and fell; bummed my leg." He rattled on while I dried his feet and wrapped them in towels soaked in boiling water, dried them, and slipped dry wool socks gently over the blackened toes. I continued the process throughout the night, knowing there was no doctor. However, we did expect one by summer.

Exhausted from lack of sleep, I dozed in the chair beside the sofa to which I had helped him. There was no way that I could ever get him up those stairs. Archie came at his usual 9:00 a.m. and was talking about leaving a bit early for the party. I had completely forgotten that invitation. I ran to my sewing machine, hoping to pick up where I had left off for the evening's celebration.

Alas, the candles had melted wax on my almost completed garment. It was already predetermined that my place, that night, was to care for George Matlock. I never finished that dress. George Matlock disliked being waited on worse than anything, but he was unable to move from his station. He particularly did not appreciate Mother's fine china chamber pot. He refused to allow me to wash his body or to touch him in any way except to dress the foot and bring him food. I sat beside him for days. Because of the steep and narrow stairway, Twiddles and Archie had difficulty when they moved him upstairs.

Archie was so wonderful, continuing to report for work daily. At that time, he was working to "insulate" the attic with moss purchased from Charley Ott at a premium price. I stayed beside George as much as possible. Archie checked on us every now and then. When I was not by his side, George could call me with Mother's silver bell, which she had used for calling servants. Of course, later it would be me she rang.

After being moved upstairs, George Matlock slept feverishly. When he did wake, ever so briefly, he saw Archie standing behind my chair with his hand on my shoulder as we both gazed down on him.

"So, that's what you've been up to," he mumbled accusingly. In and out of sleep, he would comment on how he perceived my relationship with Archie.

"You have to stay married to me. You're American only because of me.....We're partners until death.....You will never be rich with him.....You will be deported if you divorce me....Or if you marry any other..." I thought he was talking from his delirium.

Within days, our bedroom reeked of decaying flesh. It became obvious that we must get George Matlock to medical help. The nearest doctor was Dawson City, but the nearest American doctor was Fort Yukon. It would take several days to get to Fort Yukon, but it made more sense to transport him there since Fort Yukon was nearer the Fourth of July project. Nothing short of death would keep him from completing that ditch and beginning mining in earnest.

Archie said he would care for the house. I donned snowshoes for the trip. Barney Hansen carried George on his dog sled for the journey. Because the dogs had such a load to pull, they did not move with any speed. I had no trouble at all keeping up with them. Admittedly, Mr. Hansen had me ride the blades if I lagged behind, but I thought I kept up very well for a "lady of means." Ed Biederman had placed cabins every twenty-five miles on his mail route, and we took advantage of each one on our journey. The doctor was expecting us when we arrived in Fort Yukon. He had to remove two toes but said, without my care, George would have lost his entire foot.

By the time of our arrival in Fort Yukon, the sun was up. There was hope of new life as the evidence of the end of this long winter was revealed. George Matlock was frantic to get back to his July Creek project.

After his foot was treated, I accompanied George as far as the camp, stopping there for a few days to begin my list making and to prepare the camp for summer. Because the fastest travel was on the frozen Yukon River, I did not want to get caught during the River's breakup. So, when Ed Biederman stopped to drop off some mail, I tagged along with him back to Eagle.

Meanwhile, George Matlock had become impatient for the ground to thaw and started building enormous fires to begin the process. He then used nails, picks, axes, shovels – any sharp instrument – to dig at the gravel as it thawed. I made a note to make some new mittens for him. I

147

prepared a large pot of soup and foodstuffs to get him by for a few weeks, when I planned to return.

When I arrived back in Eagle, there was a telegram waiting for me from Fairbanks. Mother's health was failing and Father was requesting I come. Though Archie had taken good care of everything in Eagle during my absence, he, too, was eager to get back to his mining. Archie stayed in Eagle just long enough to be sure I had split wood for the coming year and to do a few needed repairs to the outside of the house…and to clean the chimney.

I will never forget Archie's silly look when that task was complete. His white grin was all that was visible. He knocked lightly on the back door and when I opened it, he removed his hat, revealing white skin for just about an inch of his forehead. He shyly asked for a drink of water. He was such a funny sight, I wished I had a camera that took color pictures. I stayed busy preparing the house for summer vacancy and for my journey to Fairbanks.

By happenstance, Archie and I were both traveling on the same sternwheeler as far as Circle. I would take a few days to check on George and the progress on the ditch. Then I hoped to catch the Jeffrey Quad to Fairbanks. I was eager to see Father and Mother.

I did not even consider the rumor mill when Archie and I boarded the *Whitehorse* that morning. Of course, there were others heading north along with us. Now that I think of it, I realize everyone was quiet. At the time, however, I thought nothing of it. Archie and I spent much time on the sternwheeler prattling about nonsensical poetry and memories of childhood. There was never a lack of subjects between us. The last morning on the boat, just as it pulled away from picking up a load of fuel wood and the mosquitoes were discouraged by the sudden breeze, Archie and I stood beside the railing and waved to the children whose father was

148

the wood gatherer. Then Archie turned his back to the railing and removed his handkerchief from his hip pocket and said "You have a smudge on your cheek."

I took the offered cloth and daubed at where he pointed but to no avail. Then, he ever so gently took the square of fabric from my hand and stroked my cheek. It was at that moment I realized he was the love of my life…that I had loved him even before I actually saw him. To this day, I close my eyes and smell that waft of "clean" from a dance long ago. It must have been the same for him. For, at that instant, his lips brushed mine as he tucked his handkerchief away. I had never in my life felt such longing to be held and caressed and wanted.

After I had straightened and organized the camp for the summer onslaught, I prepared for myself a pot of tea and shortbread and found a rock on which to sit for a spell. I had taken with me a book of Ella Wheeler Wilcox poetry. Reading and reflecting in the sunlight, I took the luxury of thinking about my life. It was then that I realized how truly needy I was. Both of my marriages had been arranged by Father, and neither had ever had even a semblance of affection.

Now, I understood the love poems as I read. And, as I read, I became hungrier than ever for Archie's embrace. Until now, I had not felt his arms about me except in my imagination. But of one thing I was certain—his was the love for which I had always longed.

George Matlock was in the camp when I returned. He was upset that last year's drought was raising the price of everything although the winter's snow should have dissuaded his fear of a repeat of last year. This year's worry was that he would not be able to find enough workers to complete the ditch. When the snows melted, all of the miners would certainly have returned to their own pursuits.

As I packed my belongings for the journey to Fairbanks to see to my parents' care, I placed my marriage certificate to George Matlock in the trunk, thinking *I must remember where this is in case my citizenship is ever questioned.* In the box for photographs, I placed two photographs from our wedding. Even later, as I placed them in an album for safe keeping, I was reminded that Mother was the only person present that day who came even close to smiling.

There were little hints that George Matlock might suspect me of something, but he did not come right out and say anything. At least, not right away. He did notice and comment on how chipper (my word, not his) I seemed. He reminded me, once again, that he was the connection to my American citizenship and that could not ever be changed. We did not argue; I was too submissive for such folderol.

Within one week's time, I would turn the cooking over to an injured digger. George Matlock had said he needed to go to Circle and would accompany me that far. True to his word, he met me at the boat landing, where we learned the sternwheeler was delayed. We would be waiting another two days.

George Matlock was antsy about the ditch being so very near completion. Mr. Vanderveer and some of the investors were expected any time.

"How long do you expect to be in Fairbanks?" he asked.

"I will try to be back in time for the preparations for the celebration of the ditch completion. Do you still feel the lode is that good?"

"We'll see; I'm not waiting for the boat though. I've got to get back to Fourth of July Creek. I came this far to tell you one thing. I want you to get a divorce while you are in Fairbanks."

"I cannot do that. What about our partnership? What about my citizenship?"

"You know you are forever tied to me for your American citizenship." As to partnership in any claims, your Father gave me his rights to Fox Creek as your dowry."

Jessie's Moccasins
From Jessie's Trunk

From Jessie's Photo Album

CHAPTER 18

"What do you suppose archeologists would do if they unburied my little tin box?" I wondered out loud to myself as I cleaned and dusted and sorted through what to keep and what to take to Fairbanks with me. I had saved Father's secretary until last, knowing that each piece of paper or photograph or envelope would take contemplation time.

But, ahhh, the tin box, as small as it was, held so many memories. It was stuffed full of scraps of paper, with numbers scrawled, sometimes in haste, other times very tidily printed. Yet always the same information. "1925 No. 12461 May 10th 4:15 p.m." or "1920 No. 2042 April 27 3:42 p.m." Sometimes I would have penned words like "Ice Pool" or "Breakup" on the paper, but I always put them in the tin box acquired so long ago in some distant land. Well, in 1925, I did not come any closer to guessing the time that the iced Yukon River would break up than in any other year, but I could always hope.

As I recall, to win the prize money for guessing closest to the moment of breakup of the river ice would be a major moment in one's life. In the dead of Winter, citizens of the Redmen Lodge would fill a 50-gallon drum with water and place it in an indentation chopped in the ice, mid-river; a rather sizeable flag was placed in a hole drilled in the awaiting ice. For a small fee one could guess the exact time that flag would move a given distance when Springtime arrived and the earth warmed. The nearest guess won the entire pool of money or, in case of a tie, shared the winnings. Some years are more memorable than others.

At breakup, one never knew what might float by or what possession might be lost for good, but the entire town would start watching the moment a first CRACK of the ice was heard.

The year 1925 was more memorable to me than most because it was a particularly snowy year, and because the earth warmed unexpectedly early. Official breakup occurred on April 25th at 2:00 p.m. About one week before the official moment of breakup, the earth had warmed enough that while I was gathering pussy willows for a table centerpiece the first CRACK of the ice came. Water was running everywhere and had been for several days. Rotting, porous ice was turning to fluid and running over and under the icy roads…around ice and snow berms…cutting paths through streets and yards as the water ran into the Yukon, taking with it anything not still frozen to the ground. I set my bouquet on the porch and ran toward town where I knew everyone would be gathering to watch that year's adventure. Usually nothing happens for days after that first warning sound. But that first noise is like the church bells pealing the alert of a fire. The entire town gathered in or near the Custom's Office. Some of the more hardy souls would wander off toward Eagle's Bluff for the more spectacular show. Against that enormous rock, the ice piled up higher than any tree or building I have ever seen. For several days, enormous walls of ice, as thick as most local houses, grind and crash together with a noise like a constant barrage of firing cannons. Normally, the actual breakup takes several days.

There might be a little movement visible at first, but, within moments, the ice would jamb to a halt. The process usually took several days. And, in those days, one would try to stay aware of possessions,

154

property, and even neighbors that could be carried away by the raging breakup. Erosion, flooding, driftwood, and whatever other dangerous debris the ice can carry with it are reason for watchful concern. But even with all that, the resourceful residents find treasures. Certainly, driftwood was gathered for firewood.

Once, someone spotted a Crisco can floating by. Several ladies tried to retrieve it from the raging river. In the end, it was Reverend Fullerton's wife, in her "Sunday best" attire, who was determined enough to fetch it from the icy flow. The can was a bit dented, but the key was still attached. I have since surmised that I am certain she could have somehow managed to open it barehanded. She was a very determined lady.

Meanwhile, with the warmer season came life. Besides pussy willows, the paper birch and balsam poplar would begin to show new growth. Carried with those hints of new life were the hopes of wild flowers and berries. Why, even the enormous dandelions are beautiful and welcome. Unwelcome, however, were the black flies heralding the coming of the dreaded and dreadful mosquitoes.

At the time of breakup each year, the caribou herds are migrating. Thousands of the reindeer-looking animals pass nearby, and often some will get caught on the ice floes. I remember often watching young and old caribou alike leaping from thick rafts of moving ice to a seemingly safer place only to wind up in the River. Sometimes they were able to make it ashore; sometimes not.

By the time the Yukon was completely free of ice, there were reminders of new life to come. Within days, the swallows would begin to pick homes in the banks. One could expect to see migrations of ducks and geese and swans. And the first run of salmon could not be far behind.

One knew, instinctively, the best place to be was at home; that is, if one's home was not too near the river. Fortunately, Father's big riverfront house stood probably a Fairbanks city block above the river's edge. Once, I witnessed several men trying to retrieve a small cabin from the River. One man was even on the roof, trying to row the house to shore without success.

The Yukon would flow then jam. Continuing in this routine for hours, sometimes it would break into great sheets of ice. Onshore, the snowdrifts were not yet melted through and the winter trails on the frozen streams now were swept away by the waters. Summer trails along the riverbank were still impassable even to horses and mules. I used this lull to prepare for the completion of the ditch.

It has dawned on me that the breakup of the mighty, muddy Yukon in some ways paralleled that of my marriage to George Matlock. The word "divorce" was often mentioned between us; I cannot say that we discussed it because I am not certain that we ever had any discussion on any other subject other than July Creek.

My first marriage had been annulled after Bertie returned to England. Cousin Alice wrote that she occasionally saw him. Usually, he would be in the company of much younger women. I did not look forward to a face-to-face confrontation with George. My greatest fear was of losing my American citizenship. I determined early on that I would never speak ill of George, and I have tried to fully comply with that vow to this day.

I would say a very loud CRACK came on our honeymoon journey to Dawson, not that I was ever content or happy with being married to George Matlock. And certainly no one was fooled, even on the day of our wedding, into thinking that this was a blushing Juliet and her beloved Romeo. Whether speaking of marriage or gold mining, it could easily be said of the Matlocks' "partnership" that there was little indication of affection.

Without dredging up unhappy memories, let me just say that my divorce from George Herbert Matlock was final in July 1925. The exact date I do not recall. I went to the courthouse in Fairbanks alone. Other than the judge and the recorder, no one else was in the room. I did not feel alone, but rather relieved.

I did not attend the grand celebration ceremony for the completion of the ditch. Father reported to me that it was well attended by folks who had labored on it. Even Mr. Vanderveer and Dr. Rhodius had come up from Sedro-Woolley. Several folks asked about me. Reports of the ditch's productivity were sparse, but I do know that the only time water ever flowed its full length was when it was raining, and the ditch was not needed then. Eventually, the ditch collapsed. I've been told that engineers studying the ditch later were amazed that so many people believed it would work. Apparently, a lengthy section of it was dug uphill.

Archie and Jessie

Photo from Eagle Historical Society

CHAPTER 19

On August 25, 1925, in a civil ceremony, I promised to love, honor, and obey Archie *Herbert* Mather. We vowed to stay together in sickness or health, for richer or poorer, until death should part us. How easily we spoke the words…how little we knew.

As a wedding gift, Uncle Ervin gave us a leather purse decorated with beaded flowers and the initials J. A. M. for Jessie Archie Mather. I never used the purse but added it to my treasures in the trunk. Mother gave me an exquisite bowl of my Royal Crown Derby china pattern. I embroidered a pillow for Archie "Grow old with me! The best is yet to be, the last of life for which the first was made." He made for me some shelves for my tea cups and saucers.

Father's gift did not come for six months. On February 25, 1926, the day Archie and I celebrated being blissfully happy for half a year, Father arranged for Archie to sign the papers to become the Alaska Agent of the July Creek Placer Company. It was a touching gesture.

When Archie called me "Lovee," I blushed as though I were a debutante. I was forty-four years old.

Our first Christmas together still stands as a treasured memory. Archie's gift to me was a bolt of emerald green velveteen fabric. He wanted me to make myself a dress for dancing. As soon as July Creek

Placer Company paid off, he promised to take me dancing at the Palladium in England. He also promised to build me a cottage in Eagle with electricity and real running water. I remember laughing out loud, picturing myself as "Princess Running Water."

One early April Monday, Archie left to help a friend reinforce his roof, just enough to get them through until summer. In two months they would replace it entirely. I kissed him "goodbye," and immediately set to work sorting my garden seeds for the year. I had planned to start on a new Sunday dress—something daring for me—navy blue with large white polka dots. Humming a song along with John McCormick on the Victrola, I had just cut and pressed the pattern pieces when someone began pounding on the door jamb and shouting "Mrs. Mather." It was a boy bidding me to "Come quickly; Archie fell through the roof!"

I cannot bear to relive this part of my life except to say that Archie was in Saint Joseph's hospital in Fairbanks for several months until he was strong enough to be transported to Seattle. Father and Mother and I all moved to Seattle. We were able to find a charming Victorian house very close to Providence Hospital, on 17th Avenue. From there, I could visit Archie every day for the two years he was in treatment. Meanwhile, Mother's health was failing rapidly. On March 30, 1927 she died gently, just as she had lived.

Near our Seattle residence was a charming municipal park which reminded me a great deal of Sheffield. Not only was there a small conservatory in the Volunteer Park, but on Sunday afternoons there was a band playing as children romped and young people flirted and I sat and read and enjoyed the view, weather permitting.

Father, too, enjoyed walking to the Park on Sundays. And then, I noticed he was taking daily walks. Next, the daily walks were keeping him longer. Then, one Sunday as I set my book aside to watch a flock of geese heading North, a shadow fell across my tranquil scene. I looked up to see Father before me with a lady holding onto his arm.

"Jessie, I would like for you to meet Dora Wilson." I cannot be sure, but it seems only days between that introduction and their wedding day in late March 1928. It was almost one year to the day of Mother's passing. The wedding was in the Widow Wilson's lovely house. Her daughter and I signed the marriage certificate; an Episcopal priest officiated.

Now that Father was preoccupied with his bride, I tried taking in boarders, but with Archie's needs, I just did not have the patience I needed. Finally, after almost two years, the doctors released Archie...perhaps as much for financial reasons as anything. To continue his recovery, Father gave us the money for train tickets to Archie's family in Vermont. The journey was difficult for many reasons.

Once in Brattleboro, Vermont, we were made to feel right at home. Archie and I lived with his sister and her family; his mother also dwelt with them. We all spent a great deal of time at the Mather's property in Marlboro. It was a very peaceful and relaxing time. We spent time gardening, playing Bridge, canning, reading, and discussing literature. No one could escape the topic on everyone's mind. No matter what the subject of conversation, somehow the talk always turned to the guesswork of the stock market.

Archie's health was thriving with all the attention he was getting. With his strength improving, the two of us took daily walks. It was during those walks that we talked about dreams and aspirations not realized. A journey to England was very much the topic most discussed; our problem was whether we wanted to actually move there or just go for a visit. We were happy in the eastern United States. Our social life was much more like that of my youth. The genteel manner of life was a pleasant reprieve from the hard labor of the Northwest and especially Alaska.

In late March, the July Creek Placer Company Annual Report for 1928 finally caught up with us. Everything looked very healthy with assets of $149,001. However, in the same envelope, was the obviously late 1921 Annual Report, indicating only $1.07 actual cash money and pointing to the fact that the Corporation had been in trouble almost from the very beginning. Also we were told the company was negotiating the sale of property and claim rights to R. Bauer, though he had yet to show any money for the purchase.

The more Archie and I discussed it, the more convinced we were that we needed to return to Eagle to protect our fortune. Unable to find employment in Vermont, we felt the need to be self-supporting. That meant only one thing to us – gold found on Fourth of July Creek.

Somehow, Archie's mother helped us piece together enough money and food that we were able to survive and make the long journey back to Eagle. We were able to find a family driving to California, willing to take us along in their family automobile. That was a difficult journey, with three active and screaming children climbing all over us in a closed automobile. The baby of the family could not abide the car's motion and spit up most of the liquids the mother fed him—a most unpleasant scene, not to mention the odor.

Archie and I were dropped off, mid-night, somewhere in southern Colorado and assured a bus would be coming. All I recall was huddling for warmth in a three-sided structure, the only building anywhere in sight. Someone had removed a bench seat from their automobile and left it for furniture. We laughed trying to keep it from tipping backwards every time we would doze. Waking with the sun, I found Archie had stayed awake all night to provide for me a resting place. I found, too, that we had been joined in our vigilance by laborers who did not speak a word of English—The King's or otherwise. Before the morning dew evaporated, a Greyhound bus came into sight and stopped to give us transport. Frankly, the time together on the bus provided us with opportunity to talk about our dreams and plans.

"Lovee," Archie spoke softly into my hair. "I have failed you in every way. All of my promises of a white cottage and dancing at the Palladium. Even your handsome husband is no longer. My body is so scarred and gnarled, my teeth missing, and this eye..." He grew silent.

I lifted my head, looked him square in the face, and reminded him, "You will always be my Prince Charming. We will live happily ever after. I am the last person on earth to be concerned about someone else's bad eye or unattractiveness. A cottage in Eagle will suit me fine. And dancing at the Redmen Lodge in my green attire, I will always feel like the *Belle of the Ball.* And now that you are mentioning disappointments, I suspect you might be disenchanted because I am not a wealthy heiress."

We talked of dashed dreams of ever having children, and the hope we placed in July Creek. Before our journey's end, I extracted from Archie a promise to teach me everything he knew about the process of placer mining. We talked, and I dreamed, of being equal partners and working a July Creek claim. Of course, we had to consider the fact that we had heavy medical bills. Also, it had been almost four years since we had any income. Meanwhile, bills had mounted almost beyond imagination, and our pockets were nearly empty.

We shopped in Dawson City mainly for food supplies to get us through until we knew exactly where we would be on the Creek and figured out what our needs would be since truthfully, in all our married life, we had not lived in Eagle.

Inside, Father's house was just as I had left it almost five years earlier. Of course, we dared not light a fire until Archie had checked for chimney fire danger. We were too late to start any gardening, having just missed Independence Day by mere weeks. That did not stop me from donning mosquito netting head to toe and tackling the task of weeding and shortening the head-high grass. The first thing we learned was that the project on July Creek was completely defunct. The ditch had collapsed with the first rains and no one even considered attempting its restoration. Archie and I would have to consider another source of income.

Outside, the house was in need of more than a handy man. I first noticed the erosion of the river bank, most likely caused by severe winter breakups. That would take a repair job far beyond the capability of Eagle's population and would be many years before it was accomplished. Between Archie's health problems and having been away from working for others, I found the tasks of settling back in to be a daunting endeavor.

Archie first helped Twiddles set his traps, and Uncle Ervin was gracious enough to share what little he made from the pelts. However, even Alaska was affected by the stock market crash and the years they labeled "depression." We both knew that Archie's heart was set on a quest for gold and that we surely would be better off seeking our living in gold than animal furs. For 130 days mining labor on Crooked Creek, Archie received $651.00; The pay slip I signed for being the camp cook shows I made $600. On September 14th, and again on the 15th, we received telegrams from an attorney in Fairbanks informing us we could settle our Fairbanks hospital debt for $500. Though there was not specific mention of an arrest for non-payment, it was strongly implied. I sent Father a telegram, and he very graciously sent $500 in care of the attorney. The following year, Archie worked Fox Creek almost entirely alone, with little to show for it other than aches and pains.

In late October, Fred Terwilliger interrupted our evening of radio listening at Steel's Roadhouse looking bedraggled. He said he needed help moving George Matlock's body from a Middle Fork cabin. Because of overflow on the creeks, it was late November before they could reach him by dogsled. His face had been half eaten away by weasels. His entire estate, which went to the Territory of Alaska, was $26.24.

We were able to survive, and because of Father's generosity, gathered enough to purchase a small house behind the U.S. Custom's House. It had been the Fischer's house and was in need of much work. Archie worked on our cottage every time he had a moment.

In the early 1930's, Eagle's winter population was fewer than fifty people, by far the majority of whom were the Han Nation. I am told that at one time the entire population of Eagle City, Alaska, dwindled to nine people. I know not what year that would have been. I do know there was a period of time that mail sent to Eagle was not delivered. For many years I wrote the Postmaster General pleading for the problem to be corrected. Meanwhile, my mail had to be addressed Pollack Airways, Fairbanks.

In 1935, Archie and I signed a contract with Charlie Ott and John Scheele to pay them fifteen percent of our gleanings to work their claims on Broken Neck Creek. The claim site at Fox Creek was within five miles of Broken Neck Creek, and Archie felt certain two men could pair up to work both claims. Again, I made my plea to be taught the entire process of extracting gold from the earth. Again, Archie promised me that one day he would teach me all he knew. One of the books I packed away in the trunks I sent ahead to Sitka…Oh, my! Now I am ahead of my story.

Speaking of books, it was about this time, I determined to keep a diary. As I recall, I was pretty faithful for at least one year. The diary was a Christmas gift from the Fullertons to each family of parishioners. I did not make a single entry the first year. I must dig it out and refresh my memory

165

of those years. I do recall beginning to write my daily activities and some thoughts. It was a difficult time to do so because of Archie's precarious health and the feeling that, if he left me, I would be entirely alone. This, of course makes me remember the determination of a young girl in a dark tunnel a lifetime and many miles before.

And yet, those years in Eagle hold some of my most precious memories. When not mining, Archie worked a great deal on the new rectory for the Fullertons; it seemed he was seldom home. Besides my daily routine of house cleaning, which included polishing silver and washing windows as well as scrubbing floors and staying ahead of the accumulated dust multiplied by fireplace ashes and wind and life on a dusty road, my social calendar was kept full. Daily, callers came for tea or pinochle or to read or to dine or just to visit. When I left the house, it was usually to call or play pinochle or to go to Steel's Roadhouse or Brathovds' to listen to the radio, when the program came through clearly. Every Friday night, there was a dance at the Redmen Lodge. The town Council met every Tuesday night. In 1936, I was elected to the Council with a count of 22 votes; I had never felt so popular! About this time, someone introduced a new game called Monopoly. Almost every night Eagle residents were playing the new and challenging game. I remember well my excitement when my own Monopoly set arrived by airplane.

Most days, callers would drop by for a few minutes or many hours. It was not at all unusual for them to leave in the wee hours of the morning. I remember once, our guests stayed until 3:45 the next morning; and by the time I washed dishes and put my house in order, it was 1:30 the next afternoon before I was able to climb into bed.

Often, the callers were the young ladies Nellie or Elsie Biederman or Roberta Steel. They would play cards or enjoy tea or read to me. Sometimes, I would open my trunks and show them the fine linens or postcards or other reminders of a life quite foreign to them. Of course, town ladies would drop by for tea or recipes or crumpets or a glass of Sauterne wine. I took great pleasure in serving delicate cookies or marzipan or almond-flavored treats. Those were tastes that they might never have experienced otherwise. One October, I recall a mention in my diary of a typical dinner menu when I knew guests would be coming. I prepared baked salmon, salad, string beans, mashed potatoes, bread, and lemonade, I enjoyed using almond flavoring and suspect I topped the evening meal with a cookie of some sort.

Truthfully, the majority of my callers were men. Twiddles called almost daily, often in the company of a Lodge associate. His first visit was because Archie had gone to Fairbanks to see the doctor, and Archie had asked him to check on me. I was concentrating so hard on my task of digging that I did not hear anyone approach.

A man's voice speaking, "Good day, Madam," startled me. When I turned to see to whom the voice belonged, I was staring directly into the sunlight. I was in such an awkward kneeling position and could not get up gracefully in order to remove my glove and shake his offered hand. Looking back on it, I now think the hand was offered for assistance. Anyway, I finally managed my footing to stand and offer tea. He immediately accepted with a nod and "Thank you."

I do believe that was the entire conversation that first visit. Twiddles did not particularly care for cards or Monopoly, but he did enjoy reading. I do recall one meaningful conversation. It seems to me Archie was working on the rectory, trying to finish that task so that he could get back to mining. I hardly saw him at all unless I took him refreshment. I just recall he was in town and I was feeling rather dejected.

"Oh Twiddles. I thought it might be you. Come on in. I will be just a moment." I must have been preparing cookies because I had to return to

167

the kitchen. When I turned to join my visitor in the living room, he was standing (hat in hand) in the kitchen doorway. And since my task would require coming and going, I invited him to sit in Mother's chair as I prattled on about literature or some-such subject. When I finally prepared a plate of English delicacies and covered my teapot with an Irish cozy, I allowed him to carry the tray to the dining room table.

"I thought you said you would be here later today. And I thought Mr. Fritsch was coming with you."

He looked down, took a bite of food, and waited until he had swallowed the morsel before he replied and, even then, he did not look directly at me. "I need to ask you something."

"Anything." I waited.

"Why do you call me Twiddles?"

"Oh it was just a silly moniker I attached to you the very first time I saw you…many years ago." I replied. "Why? Have I offended you?"

"You must admit, it is not a very becoming title."

"Would you prefer I call you Uncle or *Oncle Ervin* or *Monsieur Mather?*"

"Ervin would suit me fine."

I think I even wrote down in my diary to remember his name as Ervin from then on. And I did remember – for a short time. I doubt a month went by before I lapsed into my old ways, and he remained Twiddles, to only me, until his dying day.

Page from Jessie's Diary

From Jessie's Trunk

Dog Team at Riverfront House

From Jessie's Photo Album

CHAPTER 20

By 1936, Archie abandoned mining on Fox Creek and agreed with Armund Hagen, Jim Hatten, and Gust Nelson to work on Crooked Creek and Broken Neck Creek. I sat in on their meeting when all was planned and agreed upon. Once again, I presented my plea to be taught the ins and outs of placer mining. The men agreed that I could be a big help to the joint operation. As it turned out Archie stayed at Broken Neck Creek except for an occasional visit to Crooked Creek to pick up bread. I, on the other hand, stayed with Hagen and Jim at Crooked Creek. The cooking and sleeping facilities were better suited for me. So I was told.

I remember it was some time in March, around the time King George V died that Archie and Hagen readied to leave me for Broken Neck Creek. Archie had ordered and installed a window though it would still be awhile before we could occupy the cottage. He and Hagen made certain I had plenty of wood stored at Father's big house.

Their first load to the claim weighed over 800 pounds. Much of that weight was gasoline and lumber. In readiness, they had sawed lumber and moved thousands of pounds of goods and supplies to the Creek. They took that load to Broken Neck Creek, and one week later, Hagen was back for another load. For smaller loads, he could be back in four or five days. By the first part of April, things were beginning to thaw some, and Archie came into Eagle to help take a load to Crooked Creek. I was part of that load. We left Eagle at the crack of dawn and arrived after midnight. We started immediately unpacking and cleaning the cabin for use. Archie only stayed one or two nights.

By weeks end, I was preparing meals for the four workers plus anyone who happened by. It took me several days to make the camp inhabitable – cleaning the stove and straightening the bunk house for the menfolk (a word I learned from my friend Annie). I believe I was able to take Blue and go for walks almost daily. The terrain was too hazardous for me to attempt walking to where Archie was on Broken Neck Creek. However, once or twice toward shutting down operation for the year, one of the men escorted me through the cut to where my husband was laboring and came back to get me the next day.

Employing reliable workers could be one of the most difficult tasks for the miners. Take for instance the man I referred to in my diary as William. He showed up one morning at Crooked Creek, saying Archie had sent him. Be that as it may, Hagen hired him, gave him a pick ax, and showed him where and how to work on the cut. Within an hour's time, he stuck himself in the foot with his pick axe. He spent several days nursing his foot, sleeping late, and sitting and watching me work. After that injury healed, he became ill and stayed in bed for several days while I served his meals, bedside. Before the season's end, he stuck himself in his hand and repeated the first injury…only in his other foot.

My own hopes and dreams of actually being a part of the mining part of the operation were pretty well dashed. Oh, once or twice Jim showed me the sluicing operation but I never touched it. A few times, I did take a pie pan down to the creek and panned. I always got some color. But I remember well the feeling that Archie would leave me without any form of livelihood, and I would be destitute. Looking back, I was not far from right. By the time, we settled with Hagen and Gust for the summer, I had acquired the name and address of the Social Welfare Board in Fairbanks. But, now I get ahead of myself again.

As soon as the mining was over for the year, Archie went by plane to Fairbanks. On October 1, 1936, he sent me the following telegram: "HAVING THREE TEETH OUT. ALSO THE BAD EYE OUT TOO. I THINK NOTHING SERIOUS. BE HOME BEFORE LONG. ARCHIE." The operation took place on the 19th of October, and he came home with a patch over one eye. That was the Winter of the big snow.

In the memory of sourdoughs along the Yukon, there had never been a winter breakup to compare to that of 1937. The breaking ice was always forceful and not to be reckoned with. One knew better than to stand too near the river's path during breakup. This particular year everyone remembers because of the stories that are still told—stories of raging ice floes. I could always hear the crackling sounds as the mighty Yukon shifted to make room for the expanding ice. One just became accustomed to that sound. But I will never forget the sound of furious thundering that year. Even though we were in the cottage, farther removed from the river than in Father's house, we remained watchful day and night. Everyone stayed alert as enormous chunks of rotting ice moved land as well as streams of water downhill toward the River. However, the River water had spilled beyond its normal bounds, sending people running for higher grounds and even clamoring up trees.

Chief Esau had enough foresight to prepare Eagle Village for evacuation. In the middle of the night, the Chief led the entire Village populace to higher ground. Their homes and school and church were flooded for several weeks. They were able to set up tents complete with bedding and cooking facilities, and school was able to continue as normal.

I held my position on the Council for only one year. I have always suspected they were glad when my year was up. I proved to be more opinionated than anyone, including myself, would have predicted. On the other hand, another position fell to me about that time. When Customs Officer Hillard called one afternoon, he immediately informed me it was not a social call.

"Come on in," I spoke as I scurried to remove drying clothes from off the furniture. "Please, sit down. If this is something that involves Archie, it will have to wait. He is away at the moment."

"No. This call is strictly for you. I received a letter from Dr. Mertie of the Geodesic Survey in Fairbanks. He is also a leader for the Boy Scouts of America. They had been fishing on Lake Clark and somehow came up with the idea to gather books for the Eagle community. Dr. Mertie and two youngsters would like to visit Eagle and present to us the books they have collected."

"That is wonderful, but how does it involve me?"

"You are, far and away, our best-read citizen. We would like them to present the books to you."

Well, they did come to Eagle and present the books. After their visit, I came up with the idea of a library for the town. We held a public meeting with Mr. Hillard's advice, and the Eagle Public Library Association came into being.

Everyone who had books at first contributed everything they could spare. We had over 300 volumes to start with. We charged a fee of $1 for Association membership. We sold raffle tickets for a drawing to win my gramophone. Gust Nelson's name was drawn as the lucky winner. The Territory of Alaska had agreed to match our contributions up to $150 for this project. That first year, they sent us a check for $40. We raised our funds by membership fee and parties, card games, Bingo, and dances.

During the war years 1941 to 1945, the library certainly grew. Permission was granted by the Department of Justice in Fairbanks for us to use the old post office for recreation and for fund raising we had some marvelous pinochle games and sometimes Bingo. I recall that Bingo was one game that had to be shelved through some sort of law. The Eagle Public Library is probably my only legacy for my hometown.

By the end of 1937, Archie finally gave into his wretched body. He was so frail and yet made every effort to hide his discomfort. We had moved into our cottage, thinking it would be easier to keep. Certainly, with electricity it should have been much more manageable. I am not sure that was ever the case, for I found myself daily running to Father's riverfront house for one item or another. Right about this time, Charley Monk was killed by a falling rock reported to be one yard wide. I spent much of my time comforting his widow.

Archie went up to Broken Neck Creek alone. Seemingly, we were drifting apart. However, truth be told, Archie did not want to share his painful agony and chose to face it alone. He decided to travel to Fairbanks alone, and asked me not to smother him. We met for lunch at Boundary and said, "Goodbye." It was easier to speak from the heart in a public setting. We both felt certain that his journey to Fairbanks would be his last.

On December 8, I sent the following telegram from Eagle: "Bartell Drug No. 9, Seattle, Washington. Urgent rush C.O.D. Jessie Mather, Eagle, Alaska. Pollack Airways, Fairbanks, Alaska. Six one-ounce packets of each of the following. Prickly ash berries, wild cherry bark, poplar bark, skullcap. Twelve one-ounce packets valerian root, three ounce African cayenne (also bottle of best tonic). Jessie Mather."

Though Father and I had not communicated much since Archie and I left Seattle, over ten years prior, I sent Father the following telegram: "Answer to inquiry – continually in Eagle since September 21, 1936 –

Written every month – Postal authorities unable to alter conditions – send letters c/o Pollack Airways. Fairbanks, Alaska. Also parcels. Slight improvement Archie. No appetite. Low strength yet. Will you send a best tonic? – Jessie."

Archie, the "Love of my Life" was able to be at home in Eagle for Christmas. Redmen Lodge was near our cottage. I helped him dress for the evening, and had just finished straightening his tie when Ervin and Gust came by to transport him in Mr. Steel's truck. I would follow on foot after dressing myself.

Having removed the bobby pins I had worn all day, I went next door and asked Mrs. Knight to help style my hair. She followed me home and carefully wrapped my tresses around her fingers, fixing my curls into ringlets. She stayed to help me slip into my soft, velvet, emerald-green gown and to button it as I held my curls out of the way.

Once at the Hall, I sat down at the piano and played "Soldier's Joy," Archie's favorite song. As I ended the song, I crossed the room and sat down by my Archie. Mr. McW removed my violin from atop the piano and played a lovely cotillion waltz. Archie stood ever so slowly and offered me his hand, which I took. I picture us as a Renoir painting as I recall that we clung to each other without moving far from the safety of the bench. Both of us just shuffled our feet, as he whispered into my ear. "I'm sorry, Lovee. It is not the Palladium."

"Ah, no, Love of My Life. It is grander still. It is the Eagle City Redmen Ballroom. And the Prince himself has asked me to dance."

Archie's Christmas gift to me was a leather-bound book entitled *Using Minerals and Rare Ores*. It was as close as he ever came to educating me about mining. I never read the book but laid it in the trunk for safe keeping.

On January 28, I sent the following telegram to Mrs. Sam White, Fairbanks, Alaska. "Bringing Archie by Pollack plane on stretcher. Can you take him? If not please arrange removal from plane to hospital. Jessie Mather."

On March 13, 1939, I sent a telegram to Eagle from Fairbanks addressed to Uncle Ervin. In it, I informed him that Archie passed away the day before at one forty in the afternoon. "Laid to rest Tuesday, fourteenth at nine thirty in the morning at cemetery here. Will return to Eagle just as soon as financial affairs can be settled here. That may take a few more weeks. Writing next mail. Jessie."

According to the Probate Court records of the Territory of Alaska, Archie's estate consisted of the following: Carpenters tools, Miners tools, 1 4-foot buck saw (old), Gummed boots (2 pair – old), shoe pacs (2 pair, old), 3 second hand guns (Springfield rifle, 30-06) (shotgun, double barrel, 12-ga) (small rifle, 22-ga), 1 colt revolver (old), ½ interest household furniture, 2 cook stoves (old), 3 heater stoves (old), 1 oil stove (old), garden tools (old), 1 pair binoculars, 10 steel traps. Also ½ interest in mining claims on Broken Neck Creek, tributary of Seventymile Creek, Eagle Recording precinct, fourth division, Territory of Alaska and 1 cabin in Eagle, Alaska, situated at Lot 4, Block 24.

That was the sum of my inheritance.

Jessie 1942; dressed for Father's funeral.

Photo provided by Carol Knight Copeland

CHAPTER 21

It has been thirty years since Archie's death; and my heart still hurts. The precious man that I love so very much had now left me forever. My body and heart ached with an ache I had never felt. Through the years, I have lost my only brother, my parents and my grandparents. But nothing came close to preparing me for the loss I felt with the passing of "the Love of my Life." I still miss him so.

I have kept only one telegram of sympathy from Eagle. "March 13, 1939. Our deepest sympathy to you in your loss of Archie. Anne (Hobbs Purdy) & Cathryne (Knight)." If it had not been for my friends, I could not have survived the next years. Mr. and Mrs. Knight were new to Eagle themselves and were my neighbors. Mr. Knight was the manager for the Northern Commercial Company which had bought out Ott & Scheele as well as other merchants. His wife Cathryne was always thoughtful to include me on picnics or other outings. We enjoyed each other's company, and her children were good to run errands for me or make deliveries when I mended or ironed or handcrafted something for others.

It was about this time that I began deliberately giving gifts from the trunks. When Helen and Gus Douglas married, they were the only ones at the church, but the entire town was invited to Harradens afterward. I polished a silver bowl, ironed an Irish linen handkerchief and laid it open in the bowl, and wrote out my recipe for shortbread. A short time later, when Nellie Biederman married George Beck, I attended the wedding and the dance afterward at the Redmen Hall. My gift to them was a mode with silver fork and spoon for fruit. If I say so myself, they made lovely parcels, and the brides seemed sincerely pleased. When young ladies came to read to me or deliver a parcel, I would give them earrings or a handkerchief or some item they could use for play or save for another time. Occasionally, I would invite them to Father's big house and sort through my trunks with them. I knew the trunks were full of treasures far removed from their experiences, and likely they would never in their lives even see such treasures.

The crystal clock from France stopped working even before Archie's death, and Nimrod had repaired it so many times, often by crafting a part to replace the broken fixture. Eventually, I gave the clock to Sam and Helen White in Fairbanks for always putting us up, and putting up with us. I will admit to clinging to my precious china though most of it is still in the trunk. Father had kept Mother's finer jewelry.

One must wonder how I managed after Archie's death. I remained in Fairbanks for some time. It was a dreadful time for Alaskans with World War II being so near us. We lived in constant fear of invasion. In time, my eyesight began deteriorating, and I fell often. While in Fairbanks, I was employed for a time in a variety store and at the local laundromat. While working in the laundromat, I fell against the heavy tubs and broke my back.

In 1940, Gust Nelson and I decided to try our hand at mining our four claims on Broken Neck Creek. We agreed to work the claims, sharing expenses (except for food), and each taking an equal share of any expense incurred and each party taking an equal share of all gold taken out. After a futile attempt at mining, I sold my share of the claim on Broken Neck Creek to A. L. Hagen for $800.

In 1942, Father passed from this life. I traveled to Seattle for his funeral but stayed with Alaska friends and returned to Fairbanks three days later. There would be no inheritance for his only living child. In March 1943, Mr. Fullerton informed me that Ervin Mather had left me $507.19 in his will. I never saw the money but rather applied it immediately to my rather sizable bill at Northern Commercial Company.

When my eyesight was reduced substantially. I started hearing about a grand home that had been built specifically for gold rushers. At that time, there was no such facility for women, but that did not prevent me from writing to request accommodations. After being assured a room would be forthcoming, I returned to Eagle and engaged my dear friends Mr. & Mrs. Knight to help me sort and ship over 1,000 pounds of goods to Sitka. Included in the shipment were two trunks and Father's oak secretary.

In the summer of 1948, as I awaited word from Sitka, I worked as a camp cook near Rampart. I remember spending many pleasurable hours with the Sears and Roebuck catalog shopping for a wedding gift for Archie's niece. There was a lad whose father was part of the mining crew. The boy spent much of his time with me while his father was working. I taught him to disassemble the camp's wooden rain barrels to search for gold. He seemed delighted to find color left as residue in the cracks. It delighted him and kept his hands busy. As I packed to leave, I pulled from my travel satchel several books and gave them to the boy, encouraging him to be a reader.

By 1952, I grew desperate for care; I frantically corresponded with Sitka, but to no avail. They had not even begun construction on the women's wing of the Pioneer Home. Because my eyesight was so poor, I continually fell. For that reason, I stayed to my cottage. Someone—I know not who – told the staff at St. Ann's Hospital in Dawson about my situation. The Mother Superior stated that, if I was a Catholic, I could reside with the nun's in their quarters. In desperation, I signed the form stating I was a Roman Catholic. I sold our cottage to a young school teacher. He used it as an office, with another house for his family residence. Before leaving Eagle, using a black grease pen and writing with quite large strokes, I replied to some of the buyer's concerns:

§ § §

28 June 1952

Dear Alsa Gavin,

As I am writing, you are not the very lonely man from whom I received the most extraordinary letter of new thoughts for me I have ever received from anyone—not nearly as true as you seem to believe—but I will treasure just the same in my heart. I have to work every waking minute as long as I can stand up. I am so slow in getting ready for this New Life. Am trying to meet it with my chin up, but not one of the three I have will stay up.

I expect to be in Dawson for several months or until the Women's Home is finished-so really no idea. The sisters have arranged for me a room in their Residence which will be marvelous. They have an enclosed garden, and it will not be so depressing as being in a ward in St. Ann's Hospital. God is surely good, words are very futile to express the things closest to my heart.

Jessie E. Mather

§ § §

7 July 1952

Dear Alsa Gavin,

In the light of the letter I received from you yesterday, the previous one must have been a very kind piece of insincerity. To answer about the cabin: When you first saw it, it was in no shape to rent or sell as it was full of the things I had no room for here......One of the regrets of my blindness is that I did not exercise my memory enough., and there are times I am truly bothered to remember...the things I must do especially at this time of preparing for a new beginning of life and to leave Eagle...as if I had never been here and so may be privileged to live in the hearts of one or two. That, of course, I do not know. I will never forget Eagle or its people ...This is just an indigestible twist somewhere, and I forgive your discourtesy for it is not the real Alsa Gavin. God go with you and yours always.

Jessica Mather

§ § §

18 July 1952

You are right—friendship can stand many differences of opinion without impairing it – for willingly we never hurt our friends for if you should ever lose one, you die a little—for the wound does not heal. I expect to leave for Dawson this week.

I did not exercise my memory properly and gave away Father's wardrobe as well as some tools. I needed the money to pay some debts, but I must not dwell on that now.

Mrs. Hansen will read this, too.

§ § §

In Dawson, the nuns took good care of me, even filling out the forms so that I would receive public aid during my stay. I resided there with the nuns but longed to be on American soil. April 1953, I wrote to Sitka telling them I would be awaiting word from them in Eagle.

Even the President of the Bank of Fairbanks wrote the Sitka Administrator to plead my case. He was a truly thoughtful person who

183

made sure I received one fourth of a moose to help me survive. He did that at least twice.

That same month, word was received from the new President of the Sitka Pioneer Home that they would be able to take me very soon. Seemingly that worked out well, since my aid from the Yukon Territory was running out. After a little over a year in Dawson, I returned to Eagle to await word from Sitka. When Dr. John Barker, the Dawson physician who filled out my application for admission to the Pioneers' Women's Home, asked my religion, I answered truthfully – "Episcopal." However, for fear of retribution from Canadian welfare, I decided it would be best to ask Dr. Barker to change my answer to the question "What is Your Religion?" to Roman Catholic.

September of 1954, Sitka finally granted me permission. "Survival" is too strong of a word to describe my time of waiting; "endurance" might come closer. "Destitute" is probably most accurate. I was to be the second woman admitted to the Pioneer Home.

One thing that was very good in Eagle was my last Saturday. I was invited to go to the library, and they had a party for me to say "goodbye." The party was like so many I had attended for others before me. Up to that time I had been pretty emotional and I was so happy about going to the party, I didn't thank everyone the way I wanted to and I did want to say thank you from the bottom of my heart. It was so wonderful. I felt I wasn't leaving Eagle, I was leaving the presence of everybody.

First, I traveled to Fairbanks to say my "Fare thee wells" and to be interviewed on the "Tundra Topics" radio show. The show's hostess inquired about my "brogue."

"I cawn't say cawn't" was my tittering reply. I had so much I wanted to state about my life in Eagle, and I feel I wasted my opportunity.

It was dark that Wednesday morning in November when I sat apprehensively quiet in the seat to which the stewardess had led me. Seated on the plane in Fairbanks, I whispered "Ta ta, my beloved land."

******

There were six passengers plus the pilot flying the short distance from Juneau to Sitka that sunny day in November 1954. We had waited three days for the rain and Taku winds to subside; and when the weather did improve, we could not have asked for a more glorious day to travel. We were tightly packed in three rows of two seats and I was selected to sit directly against the luggage at the back of the plane. Squeezed into the tiny space beside me was Gertrude. Gertrude had been my companion for more years than I care to remember; she was faithful through thick and thin. Back in Eagle, Nellie had asked me to leave Gertrude, but I just could not give her up that easily. When the pilot saw that I was bringing along my dress form, he tried to protest. However, it did not take him long to see my determination.

I had heard, and even experienced, Alaska bush pilots over the years...after all, they had a reputation to maintain. I thought fondly of Frank Marr who had sat at my table many times and who had shared tales about me when he was interviewed on "Tundra Topics."

On this particular day, the plane was laden with tourists, seeking the Alaska adventure; I was to be the only *sourdough* aboard; and, given my failing vision, I derived much pleasure from seeing the sights through the eyes of *cheechakos*. The visitors were in no way prepared for the fright of landing in Alaska's chilly waters.

Our cargo weight was very limited. My bags, mostly laden with clothing, were just the right size for the cargo space I'd been allotted. The Grumman Goose took off from the tiny runway they called the Juneau Airport. The pilot should have announced that even though the plane left from dry earth, it was the design of the plane to be both land and sea worthy.

The time in flight passed swiftly as my fellow passengers commented with shrieks of delight at spotting bear and glaciers and lakes, sheep, and the lush scenery of Southeast Alaska. It was not until the descent directly toward the bay below that there was any uneasiness about the trip.

And so it was on that beautiful, sunny day that the other five passengers panicked and screamed from fright as the plane dived toward the water below. Then, the goose landed smoothly on the water and taxied onto Sitka's makeshift airport. As soon as the passengers' feet touched "mother" earth, they were able to laugh at the experience as they realized this would be one of many stories to share back home about their journey.

Other than luggage and Gertrude, I was last to be helped from the plane by the pilot. My feet had barely touched the ground when I heard a man's voice gently speaking, "Mrs. Mather. I am Leslie Yaw, Superintendent of the Pioneer Home. Welcome to Sitka." As I turned, he took my elbow and directed me away from the activity surrounding the plane. "We are just a short distance from your new home. Would you mind if we walk?"

"Actually, I would prefer to walk…to feel the crisp air and to smell the sea breeze…to acquaint myself with my new home. It has been a very long journey, and I am so grateful to finally be settling. Thank you so much for all you have done to arrange my stay here."

As we strolled, he explained, again as he had via mail so many times, how and why it had taken so long to establish a residence for Pioneer women. Presently, Mrs. O'Connor was their only lady resident, and she was most eager for my company. We would be sharing a water closet and kitchen but would each have our own sleeping quarters. My room was already furnished with my own possessions, items that I had crated years earlier in anticipation of this move. I had never met Mrs. O'Connor though we had common acquaintances in Fairbanks, and I had already been told that she was very lonely and loved to talk.

When we entered the building that had been established as the women's residence of the Alaska Pioneer Home, I was directed immediately to my quarters. As I entered the room, I choked back the cries that wanted to burst from my throat and the tears which were already filling my eyes. How long had it been since I shipped my most precious possessions ahead, hoping against all hope of ever touching them again? I ran my hand over the wood of the secretary, the desk where my father had spent so many hours consulting with patients.

Mr. Yaw informed me that he needed to get back to other responsibilities but that my dinner would be ready in one hour. Would I like them to bring it to me or would I like to eat with the men in their dining area? I asked to eat in privacy this once, thank you.

I must remember to ask someone what time zone we are in here. Generally, I am an early riser, but my first morning somehow I slept through the breakfast call. That was fine; I prepared myself a pot of tea; it felt so good to be reunited with my tea set and other fineries I had sent ahead. Never, in my wildest dreams would I have thought it would take so long for the pioneer home to be readied for me.

I was dressed and ready for lunch and pleasantly surprised to find men I had known in Fairbanks, and even a few from Eagle days. I was seated at a table with Mrs. O'Conner and John E. Olson, whom I had known for many years. After lunch, John E. asked if I had seen the town of Sitka yet, and when I answered him "No," several men at our table spoke up to offer to be my guide. But since John E. had offered first, and because

I knew him best, I told him I would be honored if he would show me around.

Actually, I was surprised to learn that Sitka is not much larger than Eagle, and yet they seem a world apart. The Pioneer Home is centrally located to everything, and I suspected I would not have any trouble at all learning my way around town.

In the very center of town is the Saint Michael Russian Orthodox Church, a prominent reminder of the previous owners of this land. I remember commenting, "I thought I had read it is blue?" John E. replied that he was pretty certain the one I was referring to was in Juneau, then he added, "I'm surprised to hear you can see it."

"I still have light and some color perception."

Next, we came to Baranof Hill, where the Russian commander's castle once stood. Informed that there remains only a cannon as evidence of the Russian Era, I opted to not climb the stairs. John E. drew suddenly quiet and when he spoke, it took me by surprise. He said, "I've always heard that your family was very rich and that you even lived in a castle. Would you consider it prying if I asked you about the truth?"

"I would not be at all offended, and, yes, there is an element of truth to what you have heard. However, would you mind if I took a little time to contemplate how to reply to your question? I promise one day I will answer you."

The Alaska Native Brotherhood Hall, surrounded by totem poles, and the Presbyterian Sheldon Jackson School, where Native students came from all parts of Alaska for formal schooling, reflected yet another cultural influence.

Sitka sits on an island and is surround by tinier islands still. Local shops and churches are within easy walking distance from the Pioneer

Home. Mount Edgecumbe stands out prominently as the only visible volcano in the area.

John E. said there were other sights to see, but he did not want to tire me on my first outing. There would be plenty of community activities for me to acquaint myself with the town.

Shortly after my arrival in Sitka, I received word that my favorite parson was now the Venerable Archdeacon Elliott in Fort Yukon. Immediately, I asked Mrs. Harrigan to write a congratulatory letter for me. In that letter, I told him if he decided to go to housekeeping, I could send him a parcel of dishes, linens, bedding, etc. from one of my trunks. I sent my box of loose pearls and my string of amber beads to Millie Rothenberg in Fairbanks.

A welcome parcel arrived from friends in Fairbanks. In it was my gramophone; Gust Nelson did not keep his prize but rather added it to a crate of my possessions.

I am told that I am much altered from when I first arrived in Sitka some fifteen years ago, especially my face and hair. The latter is white all over and my face is run over, but I still thank God that I have a sense of humor.

Some three years ago, I dictated my "Last Will and Testament" and signed it before witnesses. The only relative with whom I have had contact is my cousin George Fox of Gastonbury, Summerset County, England. It has been nearly sixty years since we last saw one another. I wrote him years ago that the only remembrance I have of him was as a rather dirty little boy. He wrote back to say that was more than he remembered of me.

I bequeathed my Mother's chair with inlaid pearl and the remainder of my estate to Mrs. Corrine Franklin. But, alas, she preceded me in death. She was a faithful friend, often calling on me at tea time and taking on the tasks of reading and writing for me. Now, the bank will be in charge of disposition of my possessions.

It is my desire that I be laid to rest in my emerald green dress which I made of material provided by my beloved late husband. I signed my name to my will just as I dictated it – as Jessica Elizabeth Mather. That is how everyone dear to me has addressed me. Most of those people I knew in Eagle. No harm was done by addressing me thus. After all, people whose hearts I feel privileged to have lived in gave me the name Jessica. I fold the flag of my motherland and replace it in the trunk. Perhaps I should go through the trunk's contents. Right now, I feel the need for a rest.

Jessie's Gravestone
Sitka Pioneer Cemetery

§ § §

February 22, 1971

Mrs. Betty Wyatt
RR2- Box 869
Juneau, Alaska 99801

Dear Mrs. Wyatt

We are enclosing some copies of Jessica Mather's papers that we have on file. We hope some of the information will be of help to you.

Mrs. Mather led a very venturous and interesting life. She came to the Pioneers Home with failing eyesight, and before her death she was totally blind. However, she never lost her sharp wit or her zest for life, and it was a privilege to care for her during her last days.

Sincerely yours,

Vernon L. Perry
Director

VLP:ag
Enclosures